FORBIDDEN FLESH

ALSO BY CARMEN ROSALES

The Prey Series

Thirst

Lust

Appetite

Forgive Me For I Have Sinned

Envy

FORBIDDEN FLESH

CARMEN ROSALES

Erotic Quill Publishing, LLC
3020 NE 41st Terrace STE 9 #243
Homestead, Fl. 33033
www.carmenrosales.com
Manufactured in the United States of America First Edition November 2024

Melody

I was drowning in my secret, living with my consequences.
I had one last chance at college, but something is wrong.
I can sense it in the air.
It's dark and twisted, and his name is Valen Vikiar—the notorious
bad boy of Kenyan.
Despite warnings to stay away, despite the little voice in my head
screaming at me to run, it was too late.
I couldn't resist.
I'm addicted to the rush and danger of being with him. He
consumes my every waking thought, drawing me deeper into a
dangerous game where desire and power collide.

He is evil.

I am...forbidden.

"I'm the loudest and quietest person, depends on who I'm with."

UNKNOWN

PROLOGUE

VALEN

I WALK into Dr. Wick's office, close the door behind me, and sit, late for my first therapy session of the year since the semester started. Everything is riding on this year. I'm captain of the swim team. I have to get married once I graduate to a bitch I hate.

"So you've started school, and it's your senior year here at Kenyan."

"It is."

"How are you doing?"

I grin. "You mean, how many random women have I fucked?"

"If that is how you like to refer to it, then, yeah. How are you coping with your impulsivity?"

"By coming, Dr. Wick. I cope by coming on a woman's face, stomach, or throat." I chuckle. "Kind of like you and Dillion." She squirms in her chair, but I don't miss how she squeezes her thighs. I notice she wears pantyhose that hide the little varicose veins on her legs to appear younger and the short skirts she wears just for me.

"I'm not here to discuss me, Mr. Vikiar."

"Oh, Dr. Wick. We're past last names. Except I like yours. It rhymes with dick."

"How clever. Did you think that up all by yourself?"

"I did. Did you know that a male sex addict is a master in making himself come to reach euphoria? Like your pussy, it gets wet every time I'm in here, and you begin one of our sessions, so you go back and take it out on poor Dillon, thinking of all the ways I could fuck you. I bet you think it's me sometimes fucking you with your legs over the handles of this chair spread open while I go to town on that middle-aged cunt of yours, making it come so many times you pass out."

"I think this session is over."

"I think not... I need something from you."

"What can I do for you?"

I lean my head back on the wall, looking at the ceiling. "So there's this girl..."

CHAPTER ONE

MELODY

THE SUN IS SETTING by the time I pull up to the dingy old trailer I'm renting two miles from Kenyan University.

After the second day of sleeping in my car, I was driving down this road looking for a cheap spot to eat when I saw the old trailer with a FOR RENT sign stuck on the grimy window. I pulled off the road when I saw Mr. Colby outside. I struck a deal for four hundred bucks a month, *as is*.

I turn right on the graveled drive and spot Mr. Colby working on his old car. His stringy hair barely covers the bald spot on his head. His gray beard is long. You can tell he doesn't like it, but he doesn't bother cutting it.

Brock Colby looks about to get ready for his sixty-ninth winter. He glances around the raised hood of the old car. His black pants are held up with suspenders, and his old tank top has seen better days with a stain of sweat that looks like the Panama Canal down the center.

"Melody," he says, right before the scream of shutting my driver's side door, followed by a loud clang.

"Mr. Colby," I say, greeting him with a smile.

He has grease up to his elbows from trying to fix the old Plymouth on his cracked driveway. The burnt grass fills the veined empty spaces. It looks like he's been working on the car since I was nine from the chipped paint on the hood.

"How was work?" he asks.

I look down at my red-and-white diner uniform and then meet his brown eyes. He's squinting at me from the sun's glare.

"Besides smelling like a cheeseburger, I'd say it's as good as any day."

He hooks his thumbs in his suspenders with a line of dirt under the bed of his fingernails.

"I could get you a job at the hardware store if you're interested," he says, looking down at the ground like he's thinking. "Maybe knock a hundred bucks off the rent on the trailer since you fixed it up and all."

"Oh, I don't know," I stammer.

A hundred bucks sounds like a great offer. Since the fall semester started, most of the customers at the diner are from Ohio State. I'm not making enough tips, thanks to the assholes on the football team.

I get discounted meals at the diner, which helps me cover meals, but I'm making less and less each day.

Mr. Colby smiles, his yellow teeth making an appearance, but there is a gleam behind his eyes like he's evaluating my decision. I can't be ungrateful and refuse his offer. It would be rude. Maybe he's full of shit and can't get me a job at the hardware store and thinks he can.

Once he tells them I'm turning nineteen with no retail experience, they probably will tell him they'll think about it to be nice. If he does come through, I'll have no choice but to accept.

"Alright, Mr. Colby. You got yourself a deal. If you can get me the job at the hardware store, I'll quit the diner and take you up on the offer of rent being three hundred instead of four."

"It's Brock, and don't you worry," he assures me. "You'll get the job at the hardware store. The afternoon shift until closing time," he says with conviction. "I can guarantee you that. I know you got school."

My smile falters a bit. I haven't told Mr. Crosby that I'm not in school anymore.

"WILL THAT BE ALL?" I ask, placing the check on the table.

Silence blankets the booth. All four football players from Ohio look up. My heart sinks to my stomach. Instant dislike rises in my throat like acid. I was hoping they wouldn't recognize me, but I'm not that lucky.

The one to the left picks up the check and scans it. "Aren't you that girl who got Zack kicked off the football team his freshman year?"

"I don't know what you mean," I say awkwardly.

The one with blond hair sitting across from him wearing the same Ohio State football hat smirked at me. "We know it's you; it's why we came."

"You fucked up our season that year and the one after that," the blond jock seated on the right accuses.

The person closest to the wall gives me an unwavering stare, their eyes penetrating into mine with steadfast determination. "You think you can hide from us? Zack told us how bad of a lay you were. It's why he didn't stick around for round two, and you know, had to get someone more experienced."

My face flushes with heat, and a surge of frustration rises, urging me to scream. "You have me mixed up with someone else," I assert firmly, my voice strained with indignation, before walking away.

It's sickening how they cover up for each other. All they care about is their precious football season. I thought they would let it go after I didn't report them for what they did.

"They keep giving you crap."

I retrieve the ticket and load the tray for the next booth.

I give Dorothy a fake smile. "Nothing I can't handle."

"You don't have to put up with it, Melody. I could——"

"It's okay, Dorothy."

"They can't come in here and harass you. If they do it again, I'll ask them to leave."

"I can't scare the customers away." I grab a spoon and a small stack of napkins for the couple in booth two. "I need the money," I admit. "I'll let you know when it becomes too much."

I know those assholes won't leave me a tip, but I can't be a problem for her business. My biggest fear is for her to let me go because I'm driving the customers away. It sucks, but business is business. She's not running a charity.

"I promised Adam that I would keep an eye on you, sweetheart. Boys are stupid when it comes to pretty girls."

I snort. The last thing I would call myself is pretty. I had to learn this lesson the hard way. Don't fall for a charming smile and be fooled by the wetness between your legs. It's biology. Hormones. The kind that clouds common sense and blocks comprehension.

I lift the serving tray. "That would be the case if I were."

Pfft. "You're pretty enough."

Older people say this just to be nice. To them, being young is beautiful. Like babies, no one points out how weird they look when they're born. No one says you gave birth to an alien. It's a human life. They are all cute and beautiful.

After I drop off the food at booth six, I walk to booth eight. I begin to clear the table and stack the plates when I see the bill with the exact amount. No tip.

"Assholes," I mutter, but that's not the worst part. It's what they wrote on the bill.

WE ALL HEARD YOU CRIED LIKE A WHORE

The plate rattles in my hand. A butter knife slides to the edge. A fork drops with a clank, sliding under the table.

"Shit," I grumble, placing the stack of plates on the table.

As I bend to retrieve the fork, sudden movement catches my attention—a tattooed arm sliding past me beneath the table. Fascinated, I follow the intricate design inked onto the skin, a sinister skull perched atop a hand. My senses reel as the arm emerges, offering the fork.

My nostrils flare involuntarily as the scent of a woodsy cologne engulfs me, momentarily eclipsing the smell of food.

"You dropped this," says the voice that sets my heart racing.

I straighten and look up at familiar intense hazel eyes, like pools of liquid amber flecked with touches of gold and chestnut softened with a veil of cerulean blue. My eyes slide over his gorgeous face. Straight nose and masculine lips (not too plump but not too thin). He has a symmetrical square jaw with a defined edge that complements his features. Perfect-shaped brows that could only be inherited by a beautiful woman.

His brow lifts. "Your fork?"

"Oh, thanks," I stammer, hastily taking the fork from him. "It's not mine. It's dirty. I was." My words stumble over each other.

A grin tugs at the corners of his lips, amusement twinkling in his eyes as he watches my flustered reaction.

I release a nervous breath, the fork clattering clumsily onto the plate as I hastily gather what I can from the table, desperate to escape the awkwardness. With a quick sidestep around him, I make my way to the wash station, but his scent lingers in my nose.

The man has the effect of a tornado when it touches down. You could only stare in awe as it destroyed everything in his wake, and no one could stop it.

Valen Vikiar is the swim captain at Kenyan University. Rich, dangerous, and a heartbreaker. The first time I saw him, I couldn't look away. I kept watching him from across the room. I was young and underage at a college party. People were drinking and doing things a sixteen-year-old girl had no business seeing, but I couldn't help it. At that moment, Zack was a distant memory. I had never seen a guy who looked like him.

He had his tongue down some random girl's throat. The way he kissed, the way he could fuck a girl's mouth with his tongue would make a girl reconsider watching porn and watch him instead. I didn't ask who he was, but I heard someone call his name and say he attended Kenyan University. That was all I knew about him. I have never seen him again until now.

CHAPTER TWO

MELODY

AFTER MY SHIFT, I couldn't get him off my mind. The guys from Ohio were forgotten. The note on the bill was a distant memory. I was relieved when he ordered his food to go with Dorothy at the register. I had already made a fool of myself by stammering like an idiot and knew it would get worse if I had to talk to him again.

I turn the key in the *hand-me-down* Mazda my parents bought me when I was sixteen. I was bummed when they said it was my birthday present. It wasn't because I wasn't grateful, but because I knew what it meant. I was not the favorite even though I was the youngest. My brother Adam got a shiny new truck when he graduated. My older sister, Maddy, got a brand-new Honda. I didn't complain, but I knew that out of the three of us, Adam was the perfect child in my parents' eyes. The perfect son while I was the hard-to-deal-with daughter who fucked up. I was the outcast. The one they had to make sure they kept an eye on because she didn't know any better, and Maddy was the perfect daughter who didn't cause my parents any trouble.

After Zack and his friends orchestrated my expulsion from Ohio State two weeks ago, falsely branding me as the "crazy ex-girlfriend" who stalked him, I knew I had to leave. Their disappointment was palpable, their questioning gazes piercing through me as soon as they learned of my expulsion. The weight of their accusations hung heavy on my shoulders as I packed what I could.

In their eyes, I had confirmed their worst fears, proving them right in their belief that I was spiraling out of control. It was a bitter pill to swallow, knowing that my own family couldn't see through the facade constructed by Zack and the guys on the football team. They only worried about how I could have ruined my brother Adam's future on the football team.

My brother felt bad and got me his old job at the diner after my parents wouldn't give me gas money so I wouldn't have a way of sneaking out.

Apparently, after hanging out with the rich guys from Kenyan, he didn't need the job at the diner anymore. He had a scholarship to play football and had enough money to pay for all his expenses. Then my sister Maddy moved out. She dropped out of college and left with her girlfriend for New York at the beginning of my senior year.

My parents respected her decision. They respected my siblings but not me. I was already blacklisted when they caught me and Zack fucking in my bedroom my junior year. At the time, I didn't care. I was tired of being caged. I had hearts in my eyes. Zack was my first boyfriend. He said all the right things, and I wanted to know what being in love felt like even though I didn't know what that meant.

After I convinced Veronica to take me to confront Zack when I found out he was a lying piece of shit, my life turned to dog shit. I was made fun of at school. I was threatened my senior year by the guys on the football team and the frat guys from Ohio State. I thought what they did to me right before I graduated from high school was enough. I thought it was over, and they got what they wanted. I couldn't tell my parents. I couldn't tell my brother. I couldn't tell anyone. You have to be a sick group of guys to do what they did to me.

AFTER A BRACING COLD SHOWER, I settle onto the worn sleeping bag Mr. Colby lent me from his shed, a makeshift mattress in my run-down trailer. The one that had been here before was a relic, yellowed and infested with bugs from years of neglect.

My damp hair sends shivers down my spine, a reminder of my forgotten blow dryer, left behind in the rush to escape my parents' house. It's a stark reminder of the chaos that almost cost me graduating from high school, as I barely scraped by in the final weeks, missing countless days of school.

As my phone rings, my brother's name flashes on the screen, signaling the inevitable conversation ahead.

"Yeah," I answer, bracing myself for the barrage of questions sure to come.

"Hello to you too, sis," he quips in response.

"You're calling because Mom and Dad have been blowing up your phone," I state flatly, already knowing the reason for his call.

I stare at the bold words on the bill. It's a warning. A checkmate. They haven't forgotten, and neither have I.

I pull the phone away from my ear as my brother's voice blasts through the receiver, echoing his frustration. "They have, but I'm also calling because I care. School is important, and as much as I want to ki—kick that piece of shit's ass, it's not going to change the fact that you were kicked out of school."

I notice the hesitation in his voice, catching the word he almost said. He's probably surrounded by people; their murmurs audible in the background.

"They denied the appeal. I can't go back," I admit, cutting straight to the point. It's better to rip off the Band-Aid while the wound is still fresh.

I hear a locker door slam in the background, and the silence on his end is palpable. "Damn," he finally murmurs. "That's it, then?"

"Yep," I confirm. "I can't go to Ohio State, and because I took out school loans for the semester, I'll have to pay out of pocket somewhere else. The process of appeal caused the withdrawal date to lapse, and there's nothing they could do."

"But you didn't do anything. I don't get it. They don't have proof of anything. It's all baseless," he protests.

I glance at the cracked mirror in the bathroom from where I'm sitting. "It's obvious... I don't play football, and that's what this is all about. The team, the coaches, and people with power. And it doesn't help that they have a video of me screaming and attacking him at a party the night I caught him cheating on me. It's uploaded to social media." I inhale sharply. "I don't have to go to college, Adam."

"Yes, you do. What happened to writing? You wanted to write or teach literature."

"I'll have to wait. I can go to the community college next semester. It's not that big of a deal."

"It is," he growls. "Look, I'll figure something out." And with that, the line goes silent.

I stare at the phone, making sure the call didn't drop. The plan is thirty-five bucks a month for unlimited calling, but the service sucks. I hardly have a signal out here in the trailer.

Adam has every reason to hate Zack and is stuck in a hard place having to play with him on the field, but his future is safe, and that's all that matters.

CHAPTER THREE

MELODY

THE FOLLOWING WEEK, true to his word, Mr. Colby got me a job at the hardware store. Five days a week, from five o'clock to close. It would have been great if I was still in school, but I didn't have the heart to tell him the truth.

My first two weeks at college ended quicker than it took to apply for admission. After speaking to Adam the next day, I called the school again, hoping they could refund my loans to the lender and make an exception, but I was past the withdrawal date and would have to pay the money back on top of coming out of pocket to retake the classes. I couldn't return my books either. I was screwed.

I didn't have anything to do with Zack being kicked off the football team. It was Matt and what he did to Victoria. Zack was guilty by association, and I was just collateral damage.

"Will that be all, sir?" I inquire, scanning the hammer and box of nails as the man with dark hair and freckles approaches the counter.

"I'm going to need to refill two propane tanks as well," he states briskly.

I ring him up, the card reader turning bright green as he swipes his card. "I'll need your driver's license so I can give you the key to the propane out front," I request.

With an annoyed sigh, he hands me his driver's license. I slide the key across the counter, along with his receipt. "Let me know if you need any help. Ariel would be glad to assist you out front."

"I got it," he snaps, snatching the key from the counter and crumpling the receipt along with it.

Dick.

He's not the first male customer to be an asshole when I'm trying to help. Some men think a woman working in a hardware store is an idiot.

The bell from the door rings, signaling that someone has walked in. I look up and inwardly sigh, regretting telling Adam where I am.

My brother walks up to the counter, sidestepping the *dick* carrying the key.

"What are you doing here?" I ask.

Adam looks around the hardware store. It's old and looks like it belongs in the middle of a cornfield in Nebraska.

His gaze lands on my blue polo shirt with the hardware logo engraved on the right with a disapproving look. "Why did you quit the diner last week to work here?"

"Mr. Colby said he could get me a job here and would knock a hundred bucks off the rent." I shrug. "It was a better offer."

He scoffs. "I bet. He's taking advantage of you and probably feels guilty about it. Everyone knows no one would rent that piece of crap trailer. It looks like a rotting coffin."

Adam is probably right, but Mr. Colby treats me with respect and doesn't judge. Not like my parents and not like he is right now. I can see the judgment written all over his face at how shitty my life has turned out. He's never had to prove himself to our parents. They don't question him or think his goals are stupid. They don't judge him. I've always been the one who's a problem.

"Maybe. But I have a job, a roof over my head, and I did it all on my own."

He rubs the back of his neck. "It's not a roof, Melody. It's a piss-yellow trailer with black smudge on bricks. A roof is when you rent an apartment. Renting a room in someone's house is a better option. Why don't you go back?"

"Why? So Mom and Dad can harangue at me? Tell me, 'I told you so' after they treat me like I'm some inmate in a jail cell. I can't go anywhere without them breathing down my neck. They hired a babysitter when I was sixteen," I vent, frustration dripping from every word.

"That was for your safety."

"I'm not going to stick a fork in a socket, Adam. I can eat, bathe, and dress myself without supervision. I don't need parental guidance. I'm not a toddler," I assert, my tone laced with defiance.

"I know that, but you can't alienate yourself from us—from me," Adam pleads.

"You're here." I point out. "I'm talking to you."

"Because I show up. I blow up your phone. I care," he insists.

The guy with dark hair returns with the key to the propane lock and tosses it on the counter. I hand him back his driver's license. He takes it, muttering under his breath as he exits the store.

I raise my eyebrows. "School?"

The bell from the door chimes, and Ariel walks in. Ariel's face suffers from severe acne.

According to Mr. Colby, he's twenty, and his dad owns the store. Ariel glances at Adam with curiosity but then looks away, returning to stock the shelves.

"What time do you get off?" Adam asks, staring at Ariel.

"Closing time is nine o'clock."

He turns. "I'll meet you at your..." He pauses, his hesitation palpable. "House," he says hastily, brushing off the word that nearly slipped past his lips. But I choose to overlook it, too preoccupied with the urgent question burning in my mind. I want to know how the hell I'm supposed to have class tomorrow.

"Fine. Now go before I get fired in my first week and have to sleep in my car again."

His eyes soften, and pity sets in. Pity is the last thing I want.

After Adam leaves, Ariel walks up and asks, "Was that guy bothering you?"

"Huh?"

I heard him, but I'm not sure if I should tell him that he was my brother.

"His name is Adam, right? Plays football for Ohio State?"

"Everyone knows my brother plays football for Ohio State. It's not hard to recognize him since he's the QB1."

I never got to see him play college ball after everything with Zack happened. I watched him play once at a college bar. It was a twenty-one and older joint, and they kicked me out when I admitted I didn't have an ID. I don't have a TV in the trailer or a subscription on my phone to watch him play, so I rely on the stats I find online.

"Yeah, that's my brother."

Relief washes over his features, followed by a hint of surprise. "Oh, is everything okay?"

I return the propane key to its hook. "He likes to check on me," I explain, hoping he changes the subject.

I have a hard time trusting people.

Ariel stares at me for a second too long. I always try to avoid his gaze. I don't want him to think I'm interested in him when instead I'm counting the pimples on his face. I'm not judging him for it. It's a fucked-up thing to do. He is kind of cute. He tries to hide the emo look when he's at work. He would look better if he would take care of his acne.

All the dust and dirt working in the hardware store doesn't help the cause, but I can't help it when he's talking directly at me. I count the red dots. At least they aren't infected, full of puss, or anything. I think he's self-conscious about it with the way he averts his eyes when someone stares straight at him.

The echoes of past words and actions cast a heavy burden of insecurity. It's a shared affliction, I believe, gripping most of us in its suffocating embrace. Yet the roots of insecurity vary, with each person carrying their own unique burdens hidden behind veils of silence. We all bear different scars, silent testimonies to the battles we've fought, the wounds we've endured, and the fears we dare not voice aloud.

I don't like looking at myself in the mirror.

Ariel doesn't like the acne on his face and how people might think it's gross.

"You like working here so far, right?" he says, pushing his hands into the front pockets of his jeans.

"Of course."

"If a customer gives you a hard time or anything, you can call me. I'll come right over," he says.

He's trying to be nice, Melody. Give him a break. This is work.

I smile politely. "Thank you, Ariel."

He smiles. "Anything you need"—he points his thumb to his chest—"I'm your guy," he says, with red blotches appearing over his cheeks on the last part.

After my shift ends, Ariel stands at the door while I walk to my car, taking longer than necessary to lock up. Or maybe it's all in my mind, and I'm being paranoid.

I head to the trailer three miles down the road. It's dark, with the silvery glow of the moon peering through the dense canopy of trees. I pull into the rocky driveway and spot Adam's truck.

I pull up beside him, get out, and open the door to the trailer, not bothering to wait for him to get out. I don't want to hear more about my living situation. I want to know what he meant when he said I had school tomorrow.

I place the keys on the peeled-off Formica top. I left the door to the trailer open behind me. Adam takes two steps and ducks inside.

He looks funny inside the small trailer. My brother is six-two and wide compared to my five-foot-one small frame.

I place my hand over my mouth to stifle a laugh. "Oh, you think this is funny," he says with a smile.

"I would love to see you try to get in the bathroom."

"I'll pass. You would probably have to call the fire department to get me out." He looks around. "This thing is a hazard to humans."

"It's been fine so far."

He snorts and bumps into the ceiling when he tries to run his fingers through his hair.

It isn't ideal, but no one knows where I am except for Adam and Mr. Colby. It isn't pretty to look at, but it's my hidden oasis. A place where I can lick my wounds in private.

He clears his throat. "I pulled some strings and got you back in school."

I sit on my sleeping bag. "You got me back in all my classes?"

He winces. "Not...those same classes, and it's not at...Ohio."

"Where?" I ask, confused.

"Kenyan."

It feels like all the air has left my lungs. My heart is hammering inside my chest. Kenyan? How the hell...

"Victoria?"

He nods and hands me the folder. "Alaric is one of the founders and talked to the Bedford twins and got final approval from the founding families. It was all arranged. I told them Ohio State didn't take what happened with Zack too well and how he blamed you for getting him kicked off the team."

"They made an exception for me?" I look up. "A favor?"

"Yeah. You don't have to worry about paying tuition. They have the same classes, but better. Kenyan is an Ivy League school, Melody. It's the ideal opportunity." He takes a breath. "Screw Ohio. Kenyan can open doors that Ohio could never do for you."

I look over the admissions papers. All that is great, but I've heard the rumors about the way rich guys treat the less privileged.

I have a scholarship I never applied for. Classes I never selected. It's like I never missed school. Then a thought pops into my head. The memory of *him*. The memory of his scent is like a flame burning in my skull.

"What if the guys from Ohio..."

"They can't do anything to you, Melody." He lowers his voice, like he's telling me a secret. "Valen Vikiar is a senior."

"I know who that--"

"Stay away from him, Melody," he warns. "He's changed since I first met him. He's older. He's not..."

"Not like the guys I'm used to. Victoria told me a couple of things about the guys from Kenyan."

"I'm sure she has, but not about Valen." He steps closer. "Promise me, Melody. This was the only way I could help you without involving Mom and Dad. I don't have the money for you to go anywhere else. I still have two years left before I can go pro if I get drafted or get a job."

"You didn't have to--"

"I did it because I love you. I did it because that is what an older brother does when his sister messes up."

"Gee, thanks," I say sarcastically.

He sighs. "I didn't mean it in a judgmental way. You're not the first girl to pick the wrong guy and get caught up." *If you only knew.* "I don't want you to think you did anything wrong."

"You just said I did," I point out. "You said I messed up."

He pinches his nose. "Don't..."

"Okay, fine. Valen Vikiar is off-limits," I say slowly.

"His friends, too. Scratch that. The whole swim team is off-limits. Don't go near them. They are not..."

"What I'm used to."

"If you think guys like Zack are bad, you have no idea what these guys are capable of."

"You mean Valen?"

"Especially him."

I raise my hands with my palms facing up. "Alright. Valen. Swim team. Stay away. Got it."

"I'm serious, Melody. You're a freshman, and this is your last opportunity."

"Then why pull strings to get me in if you're so worried?"

"I'm..."

He looks around the trailer, and it all clicks into place. He was hoping I would go back home if he got me back in school with a full ride. My parents would be happy, and all would be the way things were before, as if nothing happened.

"You thought I would move back home."

He nods slowly.

"You don't understand, Adam. I don't want to go back home. I'm not happy there."

"You *were* happy."

"How would you know?" I say irritably. "You were too busy at football practice and worried about getting into college. You worked at the diner to make sure you had enough money in case they didn't give you a scholarship. You didn't know what it was like for me to live with Mom and Dad when you left."

"What was it like?"

"I felt like I was in jail," I admit. "I couldn't do anything. They question everything I say. Everything I did."

"They felt like they couldn't trust you after they found you."

"Fucking." His eyes widen. "You can say it. I'm a big girl. I couldn't go on a date. I couldn't do anything."

"They didn't want you to grow up so fast."

"You mean, they didn't want me to have sex or become a woman? They gave me shit because they didn't want me to grow up at all. I had to have straight A's. I had to dress a certain way. I couldn't get a piercing. I couldn't listen to certain music."

He smirks. "You did, though."

"I had to sneak out and do it behind their backs."

I got my belly button pierced and forgot to take it off when we went to a family get-together at the lake the summer before my junior year. Everything went downhill from there. They acted as though I was addicted to drugs or something.

"I admit I rebelled, but I pushed because I felt caged."

"You were always the rebel out of the three of us."

"Thanks." He thinks I'm thanking him in a sarcastic way, but I'm not. "I'm thanking you for getting me back in school. For putting yourself out there for me. I know it wasn't easy to ask a favor from your friends."

His eyes soften. "That means a lot, Melody. Thank you."

I look at my class schedule and smile. "The schedule is good, and I can still work at the hardware store. Mr. Colby made sure I got the best shift."

Adam nods, but I can tell he doesn't approve of me continuing to work there or living here. I can't go back home. My room evokes memories of Zack, reminding me of what they did.

"Alright, call me if you need anything. Anything at all, and I'll come."

"Okay," I say with a smile. Even though I'm screaming inside because I can't tell him what they did or how sometimes I can't sleep.

I give him a hug, knowing deep down I did the right thing. As much as he thinks he's saving me, I'm saving him from the guilt if he finds out. He has a bright future. I would rather suffer in silence than drown him in the guilt of my mistakes because he would feel responsible. He would feel that he had failed me.

For a split second, I thought of turning down the offer to go to Kenyan, but he did this for me, so it's the least I can do for him. The last thing I want him to feel is that he couldn't help me when I needed him.

After he leaves, I lock the door. He tugs on the latch to make sure it's secure, and I wait until his truck drives off to let the sob gripping my throat escape.

After I take a cold shower, I sit cross-legged on my sleeping bag and rub my eyes to soothe the sting from crying.

I grab my phone. It's been a while since I've looked him up. I was tempted after the fork incident at the diner, but I didn't. It was better to assume he was like those bastards from Ohio and forget about him. He's friends with them after all. He goes to their parties, and I have to remind myself that he hooked up with girls when I was there.

I type in Kenyan University and his name. Pictures of him pop up. He has blond hair and eyes that captivate you. The kind where the world stops when you stare into them.

He's gorgeous.

I swipe and notice the pictures are almost two years old. His swimming and lap times are the more recent ones. I swiped once more and found one from last year. Shirtless. His jaw is sharper. The expression in his eyes harder. Darker. He looks older. Gone is the playful smirk he wore that night. He has more tattoos on his chest, torso, and neck. His body is hard and ripped. His shoulders are broader. His stomach is more defined compared to when he was a sophomore. His biceps bulge when he breaks through the water. There are more veins on his forearms. The look in his eyes when he thinks no one is looking, or maybe it's the pictures. People look different online than in person.

At the diner, I didn't get a good look at him. All I remember was the tattoo of the skull on his hand. I was stammering like a dork, embarrassing myself.

My brother hints that he's dangerous, and I believe him. For the first time in my life, I don't feel like rebelling and going against him.

I replay the conversation with my brother about my parents caging me at home. Maybe they sensed something bad would happen to me, like a sixth sense. The feeling you overhear parents talk about when they predict how their kids will turn out if they don't discipline them in a certain way.

I didn't listen when they said to stay home and not go out, not to trust boys, or to do things without their permission.

I wasn't supposed to confront Zack that night. The plan was for me to remain at home. I was angry that they hired Veronica to babysit me like I was a child. At the time, I thought it was stupid. Maybe it was, but I convinced Victoria to take me to confront him at the frat party.

I was angry and stupid. I didn't think anything bad would come of it. I was pissed off like any girl my age would be after a boy lied, cheated, and risked your parents' trust. I was excited when the popular quarterback said I was pretty. He had me wrapped around his finger, with stars in my eyes. At school and at his games, he kissed me every time we were together. He said he would wait until I was ready. He wasn't like the other guys. Everything was perfect until I allowed him to sneak into my room and let him fuck me. He had me when he said I had a beautiful body.

When my mom walked in on us, it was too late. The deed was done. He practically flew out of the window. It was awful. My parents, and to be honest, the sex. I didn't feel anything I read or heard about. No butterflies fluttered in my stomach.

The next day, he bragged about it with his friends. All the things he said to me before were bullshit. He said I was it for him. That he never met a girl like me before. That I was different. It was all lies, and I fell for it.

If your parents warn you about boys, listen. If they want you back at a certain time, listen. If they tell you that you are too young for something, listen. Because when shit happens, it's too late to go back.

Don't trust a man when he says you're beautiful. It means he wants something from you. When things don't turn out the way he planned, he does something worse.

Like Zack did to me. He did the unthinkable. He didn't care if I stopped breathing or if my hands shook. He got what he wanted.

Now I feel useless, drowning in a sea of my own tears from the pain and rejection.

Everything I felt came in an exact order after he fucked up my life.

After the lie, the consequences.

After the consequences, the pain.

After the pain, the tears.

After the tears, the damage.

After the damage, nothing is left, and I can't go back to the way I was.

It's too late. Now, I'm someone else.

CHAPTER FOUR

MELODY

I'VE NEVER BEEN on Kenyan's campus before. It has a Gothic Revival-style that was popular in the 19th century. I widen the picture of the school map on my phone with two fingers to try to find building four. I walk past the old cemetery, hoping I'm heading in the right direction on the narrow cobblestone pathway through campus, bordered by rows of ancient trees whose gnarled branches cast eerie shadows upon the ground.

Despite its age and aura of mystery, the campus is a bustling hive of activity. Students hurry to and from class.

A magnificent cathedral-like church with pointed arches, stained glass windows, and flying buttresses dominates the campus. It looks like they conduct rituals instead of prayer inside.

I have to admit, the campus is beautiful. The leaves and trees add to the effect. It looks like I'm inside the set of a fictional novel where this is a school for vampires and werewolves.

Massive, aged stone buildings stand above, their spires extending upward like fingers stretching to the sky. It's old but prestigious.

Graduating from Kenyan is like graduating from any other Ivy League school, except you are guaranteed a job through connections. There is no fancy football team like in Ohio. Swimming is the sport of choice, and its legacy is their culture. I'm sure it's due to the history of the school.

I look around to familiarize myself with the campus.

I check my phone to see what other places it has to offer wishing I could stay in one of the dorms. I locate a local spot on the map named Babylon, marked with a food symbol.

I turn left and make my way around the buildings, bypassing the female dorms, followed by the male dorms.

One guy walks out in front, pauses for a second, and gives me a once-over. He nods, but I ignore him and keep walking. I turn right until I see the neon sign and cross the street.

The place is buzzing once I'm inside. Students walk in and out of the exit, laughing with their friends. Others replace the spot they just vacated.

This is a Kenyan hangout. The school's accolades hang on the walls. The school insignia and past presidents. The numerous swim championships and famous people who have graduated from here.

I scan the rest of the place. It looks like a dive bar. Pool tables are to the left. College kids occupy the four arcade games available.

"Comedown" by Bush is playing from the jukebox. People form a line for drinks on the left side of the bar. The booths are all taken except the one for three to the right in a secluded corner.

A lady walks up with pink hair, a short skirt with holes in her tights, and combat boots. She appears to be the hostess with the way she keeps waiting for me to say something.

"Table for one," I tell her.

She nods, points at the empty booth, and hands me a menu. "Someone should come by to take your order. In the meantime, you could get yourself a drink at the bar and take it to your table."

"Thanks," I say, taking the menu.

I don't want to look stupid and order a soda or a glass of water at the bar. I don't have a fake ID, and this place is right off-campus. I'm sure they will ask me for one.

I sit at the booth and people watch. I thought it would be a good idea to scope out the campus and see where everyone hangs out. What they're like and what I should expect. I'm glad I did. The people here are nothing like the normal college students from Ohio or any other college I've ever seen.

It's like watching college students in a time machine. Alternative rock styles—emo, goth, and preppy—from the 1980s and 1990s are evident among the people walking around. The way they wear their clothes. Different hairstyles exist. You can tell the people here are all from different places, but one thing doesn't go unnoticed: social classes. You can tell who comes from money and who got lucky for the opportunity to go here.

My eyes scan the pool tables when a group of girls walks over, and then I see him. He's hard to miss from any distance. He's leaning over the pool table in concentration and taking a shot to the corner pocket.

The muscles of his arms bulge when he pulls the pool stick with his hand, sliding it between two fingers. I can't make out the color of his eyes because it's dim. My eyes admire how strong his back muscles are and the way they flex when he hits the ball with the pool stick.

"Valen," someone says. I look over, and a girl with soft pink hair slides on the bench in front of me. "Sorry," she says with a smile. "I saw you sitting here by yourself and figured you could use a little company. My name is Rose, by the way."

I don't, but I don't want to be rude.

"I'm Melody."

"You're new here." She squints her eyes like she's figuring me out. "Freshman."

I don't confirm or deny—it's not hard to guess, especially since I don't have a beer or cocktail in my hand. My gaze swings back to the pool table just as Valen takes another shot. Girls gawk at him from the other side, their cheers echoing the balls smacking together.

His smile lasts only a fraction of a second before a serious expression wipes it away. There's something powerful about watching him without his knowledge as if I'm observing through a looking glass.

"You like him?" she inquires, her smile betraying her interest.

My eyes snap to hers. "No."

I don't know him. He's nice to look at. It's normal for a girl to appreciate a good-looking guy.

Her smirk deepens. "Oh, come on. Every girl finds him hot. The problem with him is," she continues, lowering her voice enough that I can hear her over the music, "he doesn't want anything to do with a girl once he's done. No girlfriends. No relationships. He's just a hookup."

"And you," I probe, my interest piqued. "Do you think he's hot?"

She pinches her brows like I'm blind. "Of course, I think he's hot. Valen is the hottest guy on campus. The last of the sons of the founding fathers. I heard the others married right before graduation." Her gaze flickers briefly toward the group of guys talking to Valen, then back to me with a hint of skepticism. "But Valen. I don't think he's the type to settle down." She leans in. "I heard he's a good fuck and doesn't plan to slow down. I mean, he's fucked all the hot girls on campus. Two, three, sometimes four at the same time."

"You mean orgies. Did you sleep with him?"

She shrugs, a playful laugh escaping her lips, igniting a flicker of jealousy within me. "If you want to label it that way, sure. And no to your second question. He definitely has a preferred type."

A wave of relief washed over me when she admitted she didn't sleep with him. I think about Jess and what Veronica said about her. She was the closest Valen ever came to wanting something serious with someone, but she married his friend instead. That means she fucked them both. Rose says he has a type. Jess was blond, but I don't want to tell her that because that would mean I pay attention. It would mean I care and I'm interested.

Rose is pretty but is on the skinny side. You could tell by her arms. They are very thin, like a person who has an eating disorder. I'm not one to judge, but she would look healthier if she ate a little more.

"What's his type? I don't really care, but there is no one here right now that is interesting to talk about, so enlighten me."

"Nothing that resembles me," she replies, her eyes losing some of their brightness. "I'm too skinny. Back in high school, guys would tell me, 'Go eat a cheeseburger.' Some think I'm pretty but too bony. I think they were trying to be nice."

"I'm sorry," I say, knowing firsthand how that feels.

She waves her hand like it's no big deal, but I can tell it is. It's a very big deal.

"I think he likes blond girls. I heard he liked this blond girl his sophomore year because he was around her more than the others. I think she was the only one he slept with more than once, but the other guys were here around that time until they graduated. They were older, and now it's just him."

I turn my head and catch a girl whispering in his ear, but his expression is hard as if he's annoyed.

"Who's that talking to him?"

"That's Melissa. Senior. Stay away from her. They have something going on that no one knows the details about. She loves to play games, and according to some of the girls in the dorms, she's bi and loves pussy."

I raise my brows. "You think they..."

"Oh yeah." She nods. "They've known each other since high school. She comes from money. Her dad is some investor, I think, or an exporter. I'm not sure, but her family is connected. She's a real conniving bitch and loves his leftovers."

"Leftovers?" I ask, confused.

I knew Veronica didn't tell me the whole story, but this is new. This is weird. This entire school and the people who go here are fucked up. It's like opening Pandora's box and finding a whole lot of dark and crazy.

"She fucks all the girls he fucks. It's a game for her. I'm not sure if they still sleep with each other, but I think he's annoyed by it yet does nothing about it. Rich people shit."

"And you?"

"My sister graduated last year, and I was able to get a scholarship."

"That's impressive. It sounds like she got something worthwhile from this place."

"Sure, if you overlook what she went through."

I'm about to probe further when the server arrives. I order a basket of fries and a Coke. She opts for a Sprite. Once the server departs, she leans in slightly.

"She left with more than just a degree—and also a broken heart."

I nod, sensing the weight of her words. Curiosity piques me, but it feels too personal to pry.

Her gaze suddenly fixes on a new arrival. "See the jerk at two o'clock? That's Garret. The very definition of a rich asshole. Throws wild parties when his parents are out of town. And yeah, that was the one who shredded my sister's heart. He slept with her, then pretended she was invisible. Just another reason to stay away from them."

"I know. I heard," I say insentiently.

"I hope they drown," she teases.

I can't help but chuckle. "I heard demons can breathe underwater."

"You're kinda funny. Which dorm are you staying in?"

"I'm not."

"Ah, rich parents, then?"

"Hardly. I live off-campus. I could only score a scholarship for tuition."

"That's rough."

"Yeah. It's because I'm a transfer from Ohio."

"Ohio State?" Her tone registers surprise.

"The very one."

Her curiosity deepens. "Why did you transfer?"

A wave of discomfort washes over me, a pang of regret for letting that detail slip. I fidget with my fingers, trying to keep the burgeoning memories at bay. It's like trying to peer through a dense, black curtain.

The arrival of the server with our food is a welcome distraction. "Who else should I steer clear of?" I ask, eager to shift the focus.

Rose's attention locks on something—or someone—behind me. "All of them," she states flatly.

I sneak a glance back. Garret fixes his gaze on Rose, giving his gaze a hard edge. Off to the side, Melissa is gone. Instead, a blonde stands in front of Valen, her back to us, clad in a skirt that leaves little to the imagination, deep in a one-sided conversation. Valen's gaze is adrift, ignoring whatever she is telling him.

Then as if drawn by some silent alarm, his eyes meet mine. I hold his stare, finding an unexpected steadiness within. The sensations that once fluttered through me at the sight of him are conspicuously absent—no butterflies, no tinge of envy.

My brother's voice is telling me to stay away. Rose's warning —they've doused any spark that might have lingered.

The girl places her hands flat against Valen's chest, her red nails making a vivid proclamation. He glances at her hands, then returns to me. Redirecting my attention, I join Rose in focusing on the fries.

"He hasn't looked away," Rose murmurs, her voice low after taking a sip of her Sprite.

Whether it's recognition or curiosity in his eyes, I can't distinguish. So I dismiss it, saying with casual indifference, "He's probably wondering why I was staring."

She sneaks another peek. "He's still watching."

I place the fries back in the basket, my fingers brushing the napkin to rid them of grease. "Excuse me for a moment. I need the restroom."

Desperate to divert the conversation away from him and to avoid the temptation of looking back, I slip out of the booth and make a beeline for the restroom marked "Females Only."

Inside, after using the handicap bathroom and washing my hands, a scream pierces the silence as the door swings open. I pause, waiting for the newcomer to choose a stall so I can leave discreetly. Tilting my head, I try to catch a glimpse of their feet but see nothing. After a fruitless minute, I unlatch the stall, and the world plunges into darkness.

Panic surges as I blink, futilely willing the lights back on. "Hello?" My voice echoes. "The lights are off. Could you turn them back on, please?"

Silence is the only reply.

Enveloped in darkness, my eyes fail to adjust. Footsteps creep closer. I lurch out of the stall, colliding with a wall—someone. My hands shoot up, grasping at empty space.

"This isn't funny," I snap, my nerves fraying. "What the hell?"

A single "Shh..." sends a wave of dread through me, heavier than the darkness itself. I'm trapped. Each attempt to move is blocked.

"Is this some twisted joke, some freshman hazing?" My voice is a mix of anger and fear, the latter winning as I'm met with silence, thick and unyielding.

Memories of that horrific night begin to replay in my mind, my ears ringing with the echo of that night. Then, mercifully, the door creaks open, casting a feeble strip of light from the hallway. But there is no one.

I fumble along the wall, my fingers finally flipping the light switch. I wince as the harsh fluorescent lights flicker to life, taking a moment for my eyes to adjust. Tentatively, I look into the mirror and freeze. Scrawled across it, written in red:

WHO SAID I WAS A GIRL?

CHAPTER FIVE

MELODY

I MAKE it to building four and walk into the creative writing class I'm assigned to. I look around the stadium-style seating to find an empty seat. I tried to think about the message in the mirror last night. It must have been a prank, but what if it wasn't?

Adam texted me this morning to make sure I showed up to class and asked if I needed anything. He assured me that I would be able to catch up and the professor would allow me extra time to submit any missing assignments. I hope he's right.

I was going to call Victoria this morning but decided against it. I didn't want to make a big deal about what happened in the bathroom at the bar. I wouldn't know what to ask her. What would I say? Hey, Victoria, did girls from Kenyan act like psycho freaks, turning off the bathroom lights and trying to scare people while they were using the bathroom? She would think I was crazy. She's married to the love of her life and is happy. She doesn't need my baggage to cloud her mind. Knowing her, she would want to meet up to check on me, and I would have to lie to her too. She would want to know how I've been, if I'm dating, or if I have any friends. You can tell only so many lies before the cracks in the truth begin to surface. Knowing her, she would see them. She would sense something was up.

Students file in and take their seats. I choose a seat in the top right corner, away from everyone but where I can *see everyone.*

A man walks in with a suit and tie and a Starbucks coffee in his hand. I can only gauge that it's the professor. A huge contrast from Ohio. He looks like he belongs at a law firm in New York

City. Like those guys in the show *Suits*. Black suit, white shirt, light blue tie, and haircut parted on the side.

I notice everyone pulling out a composition book, so I take out a blank sheet of paper. I make a note of what is required for each class and hope I have enough in my account to cover it.

A group of guys walk in; you can tell by the way they draw everyone's eyes that they are popular. Even if they weren't, their looks are enough to take notice. They are good-looking, and judging from the shirts that read *Don't Drown*, it gives it away.

The girls seated closest to the door stare. Some giggle. Some whisper among themselves. The door opens, causing the room to feel devoid of air. Everyone's head lifts, and conversations stop. The sound of my heartbeat pulses in my ears. It amazes me that he's in this class. Not because it is a writing class. It is an elective, which means seniors and freshmen can take it. What surprises me the most is that *he's* in this class with me.

Valen Vikiar.

I swear my heartbeat slows down when he walks farther in the room and then begins to beat frantically when he takes a seat on my side next to his teammates, but I'm relieved that I chose to sit in the last row where no one is seated next to me and I have a clear view of them four rows below me.

The professor looks down at the podium.

He clears his throat. "Before we begin, we have a new student who transferred in from... Ohio State but missed the first two weeks of class due to a family emergency." My stomach clenches. These people are better liars than the devil. People *boo*.

"Settle down, settle down," the professor says, "none of that. She saw her mistake and is now doing the right thing." I roll my eyes at the jab. "Miss Melody Price," he calls out, and he scans the room along with everyone else. A set of hazel eyes meet mine, causing the room to sway before my eyes. I didn't think he noticed I was here.

My brother must have talked to him. I didn't think he knew

who I was. He's never said two words to me. I feel like the new kid in elementary school.

I shift in my seat. "Here," I say, loud enough for every pair of eyes in the room to land on me.

"There you are, Miss Price. Welcome to Kenyan," Professor Owens announces, his smile failing to mask the undertone of formality. "If you need to catch up, feel free to partner with someone or see me after class."

"I'll do it."

"Ah, Mr. Vikiar. How noble of you," the professor says with a touch of sarcasm.

All eyes dart between Valen and the professor.

Slowly, Valen's smile unfolds, a calculated display hinting at the sharpness beneath his exterior. "We both know there is nothing noble about me, Mr. Owens."

Everyone laughs. The professor turns bright red and looks uncomfortable. I press my hands into my lap. Shit.

"Of course. Uh, Mr. Vikiar." Professor Owens gives me a sympathetic smile. His smile tells me I have no choice but to get the missing assignments from the devil himself. "Miss Price, Mr. Vikiar is volunteering. You will find that he is always erudite. He's a senior and is well-informed about the material."

"Good to know. Thank you."

My brother's warning about him goes off like an alarm in my mind. The room's focus returns to the professor, yet a palpable tension persists, akin to the quiet before a storm. Amid the sea of faces pointedly focused on the lecture ahead, I dare to glance to the left. My breath catches. The air between us crackles. Valen's eyes meet mine, his look piercing and unyielding, a silent challenge that leaves the weight of his attention both unsettling and undeniable.

As the professor begins the day's lesson, all I can think about is the way he looks at me. It's like he can see inside me. Like he's rummaging in the dark, knowing where everything is, and making sure everything is where it should be. Or maybe he's trying to intimidate me because I messed up, and my brother needed a favor for his wild little sister that he can't keep out of trouble.

I stare right back.

My junior year in high school, I thought he was a god the first time I laid eyes on him at the college party. After my sister, Madison, stopped me from tearing Zack and that tramp's eyes out, I wasn't aware I was fighting for a boy who would end up ruining me.

Not when I was lost in hazel eyes across the room. Eyes that told me I was fighting for the wrong guy. I was mesmerized by how gorgeous he looked, but at that moment, I begged him with my eyes to take me with him.

I was confused. It wasn't my sister who got me to stop. It was him. I knew he was older since he was at a college party, but I didn't care. I didn't even care if he had a girlfriend.

In those days, I was fearless. I wanted to explore, have sex, and fall in love.

All it took was one look, and he had me.

Too bad I'm not the same stupid girl he thought he could fool.

I watch his tongue rub slowly over his piercing on the corner of his lip. Any girl would fall for him. He is sexy. I don't miss the way the girl to his right sneaks an appreciative glance every few seconds. He must be used to the attention. In the diner, at the party, in this classroom.

She isn't the only one sneaking a glance at him or giving him a knowing smile. His eyes are telling me what I don't need to ask. He's fucked almost every girl in this room, but I see something they don't. I see a face on the other side of the mirror.

There is always a Jekyll to Mr. Hyde. An ugly side to a beautiful one. Valen has both, and no one realizes it until it's too late.

Once the other side appears, run.

After algebra, I walk out to the quad. I take a seat on the bench at an empty table and pull out a bag of chips and a can of Coke I purchased at the gas station for seventy-nine cents, compared to two dollars and fifty cents on campus. It isn't much, but it's what I can afford right now.

I pull out my schedule for my other three classes when I feel the bench vibrate. A shadow falls over the paper in my hand. I look up and see the same group of guys from earlier in the creative writing class. The guys on the swim team.

"It's the new girl," the one with brown hair and brown eyes says.

I pop a chip in my mouth and ignore them, hoping they will go away or ignore that I'm here.

"Leave her alone, Charles. You can tell she doesn't like dick," the guy with dark hair seated to his left says.

The other two chuckle. "Yo, Garret. Where's Valen?"

That has my head snapping up at attention. My eyes land on Charlie. His eyes gleam with amusement. "Hmm, we have a winner. I'm not surprised, though."

Garret walks over and sits next to Charles. I remember my brother mentioning his name around Victoria once. She said he was nice. He wasn't a bad guy.

Garret's dark green eyes meet mine, and he says, "Leave her alone, Charles. I know her brother."

Curiosity washes over Charles's expression. "Who's her brother?" he asks, looking straight at me.

"Adam Price. Quarterback for Ohio State That's his little sister," Garret replies.

"Shit. I thought you were the other one," Charles teases with a wink. He leans over the table and whispers, "The one who likes pussy." My jaw tightens.

I hate the way he talks about my sister. Joking about her sexuality and assuming I was her.

The other two guys sitting on Charles's right look at me with a glassy type of interest.

"Charles," Garret says in a warning tone.

I feel the bench vibrate again, and then someone slides into the seat to my right. I don't have to look to know it's him. I can smell him. There is nothing like it. His distinctive scent stays in my nose and refuses to leave, like a memory.

"Having fun, Charles?" Valen says with an edge to his tone.

The chips I ate turn into a ball at the bottom of my stomach. I'm not sure if he's mocking him or angry that Charles is giving me a hard time.

"I was getting to know the new girl. I figured out what she likes," Charles says with a smirk.

"And?" Valen asks, like he gives a shit what he thinks. Talking about me like I'm not sitting here is not rude.

Charles lets out a nervous breath. "She likes...dick."

I stand, having heard enough. The last place I want to be is with a bunch of guys who have the power to make me disappear. I need to leave.

Valen looks up, and our eyes meet. "Sit," he commands.

It's the first time he's said anything to me. He doesn't introduce himself and isn't polite. He's an asshole, just like his friends.

I grab my bag, leaving the chips and can of soda on the table, and turn to Charles. "Fuck you," I spit, and I walk away.

Laughter trails me, but I don't look back.

I WALK into the hardware store for my shift, glad I didn't run into *him* again. I make my way to the back, where there is an old punch-out machine drilled into the wall. I take the brown card from the slot, hear the stamp, and place it back.

I didn't think businesses used these anymore, but this store is old. I'm surprised they have a card reader to accept payments. I walk to the only register to relieve Ariel so he can stock shelves and help customers on the floor.

"Hey, Melody. How was school?"

I pinch my brows in confusion because I didn't tell anyone I was going to school today. I found out last night. How would Ariel know?

Ariel reaches behind me and grabs a bag. "This was delivered right before you walked in." He holds up the takeout bag, and the smell of french fries drifts toward me from the diner. "There is a note."

MELODY, CALL ME FOR THE ASSIGNMENT 614-233-6708.

"Oh," I say, taking the bag.

"I figured you were in school because of the note attached."

I open the bag, pulling the handles apart, and the staples give way. There is a cheeseburger and fries with the same brand of soda I left on the table, along with a brand-new bag of chips.

I look up. "Who dropped this off?"

I know who it's from. But how did he know where I worked? I never said a word to anyone. He doesn't know me, and I don't think my brother would be stupid enough to tell him I worked here.

I stare at the number like it's a creditor out for blood. Valen knows I need the assignment to pass the class. But why didn't he write the assignment down on a piece of paper and slip it inside the bag instead of having it delivered?

I was told to stay away from him, but how can I if I have to call him for the assignment?

Ariel shrugs. "I was in the back. I heard the bell above the door, and by the time I walked by the register, it was here. I didn't see anyone."

I look into his eyes to see if he is lying, but I don't know him enough to know for sure.

When I get home, I type the number four times on my phone, delete it, and start over. It's my sixth time entering, and if I want to catch up in the class, I have no choice but to call. If not, I would have to explain to the professor why I couldn't get the assignment from him.

I stare at the numbers on the screen, the pad of my thumb hovering over the keyboard. I look out the small window at the dark sky. A cloud passes over the bright moon.

It's just a text, Melody.

He probably won't text back right away and wait until morning. I'm sure he's hanging out with his friends or with a girl.

"I'm losing my mind," I mutter.

It's not like I'm going to hear his voice or anything. He might not even recognize the number and leave me on read.

I let out a puff of air. My stomach turns into a knot.

Melody: Hey.

One.
Two.
Three.

I hit send and wait, staring at the screen like a bomb about to go off.

He's not going to reply. It's taking too long. I'm about to place my phone on the charger when it rings.

The phone slips from my hand and falls to the floor with a thud.

Shit.

I pick it up and look at his number flashing on the screen.

Oh. Fuck. I was expecting a text, not a phone call.

I hit accept.

"Hello," he says darkly.

Fuck. His voice sounds sexy over the phone.

"H-hi. Um, this is…"

"Melody," he says.

He knows it's me. *Hey* could have been sent by anyone. A random girl he slept with. He's rich, gorgeous, and popular.

Get a fucking grip, Melody.

He didn't give you his number to ask you out on a date.

"Yes," I say breathlessly. "How did you know where I worked?" I rush out.

I squeeze my eyes shut. My heart is pounding. I'm hot. My hands are sweating. I can't believe I said that.

"I took a wild guess," he says, but we both know it's a lie.

The more he talks, the richer his voice is. Deeper. Darker. It's not playful. In the back of my mind, I don't remember him being so serious. So brooding. I thought he was putting on a show in the quad and the classroom, but he isn't.

"How?"

"It's not important right now. It doesn't change the fact that I know, does it?"

He's right. So what if he knows?

"Why?"

"Why what, Melody?"

"Why did you volunteer? Why did you buy me food?"

"Because I want to, and I can."

"What's the assignment?"

The faster I end this call, the better.

Sweat drips down my neck. I need fresh air, but I don't want to go outside in the dark or turn on the small air conditioner.

"How was the food?"

"It was good. Thank you," I stammer.

"Hmm, it's a shame. I would have loved to see you eat it."

"A cheeseburger?" I ask, confused.

Who the hell wants to see someone eat a cheeseburger? They're big. Greasy. Messy.

"I would have loved to see how wide your mouth can go when you take a bite."

Oh fuck. I squeeze my thighs together. My inner thighs are wet, and I know it's not sweat. I'm wet and aching.

"You like to watch people eat? Is that your thing?"

He chuckles. "I want to watch *you* eat."

"That's kinda...weird."

"Would it be weird if we both watched each other eat?"

"That wouldn't happen," I say quickly. "What's the assignment?"

"I have to see you to give it to you."

"Why?" I ask, confused.

He could just tell me. Why is he playing games?

"It's complicated."

"It can't be that hard."

"It's better if I tell you in person."

I sigh. " Fine. You could give it to me the next time we have class."

"How about lunch tomorrow? Meet me at the quad, same table."

On campus. Nothing can happen to me on campus. There are students everywhere.

"Alright," I agree.

"Noon, Melody."

"Alright," I repeat.

I pull the phone from my ear to hang up.

"Melody?" He says my name slowly.

I place the phone back in my ear. "Yes."

"Be there; don't make me find you." And he hangs up.

I stare at the phone like he's going to crawl out of it and grab me.

What the hell have I gotten myself into?

CHAPTER SIX

MELODY

AFTER HISTORY CLASS, I walk toward the quad through a river of students. Some give me brief glances that are sharper than glass. Knowing grins flicker across faces, igniting a trail of anxiety that coils in my stomach. My hands get clammy waiting for the laughter that doesn't come, or is it something darker, a prelude to a torment I can't see?

I'm paranoid. I have anxiety. Get a grip, Melody. It's not going to go away. Deal with it.

I grin back, refusing to show my inner turmoil. I have to stop thinking about the past.

But when I arrived on campus, I changed my mind. I thought I was crazy to even think I could.

What if they know people from Ohio? My brother knows Valen and the other sons of Kenyan. They go to parties, hang out, and date. It's not uncommon. I've seen it with my own eyes. Other people from Kenyan could have been there that night or heard the rumors they spun about me. Even recognized me the same way Valen did.

I push the doors to the exit. The wind is cool against the skin of my cheeks. The sky is overcast. The church looms, casting a shadow on the cobblestone pathway leading to the tables. The wind causes the trees to groan and drags the leaves across the grass.

A sign that fall is coming.

My throat goes dry when I spot Valen sitting on the bench. My steps slow, giving me time to look at him before he spots me walking over. Charles sits across from him facing him. Garret is saying something I can't make out.

My eyes slide over the tops of his tattooed hands, roaming over his face with a predacious smirk aimed right at Charles.

Getting a good look at Valen, the pictures don't do him justice. Every time I see him, I find something else that is perfect. You could stare at him for hours, trying to find a flaw, but would come up empty. His jaw is more defined. His shoulders broader. He's not as lean but bulkier. He put on more muscle, and you can tell by the definition of his shoulders that he's strong. His messy blond hair and lip piercing add to his appeal. I observe that he has painted his nails black. His bottom lip is a shade darker than the top.

My boots sound like bricks hitting rock with every step I take. The crunch of leaves with every stride. Hazel eyes, with a hint of blue, land on me. It feels like a hammer hitting a high striker at a carnival game right to my brain. His eyes drop to my black boots and slowly rise, pausing by the hem of my skirt like he is waiting to see if I'm bare or wearing panties.

As I approach the table, my gaze immediately finds Charles, my hand flying to cover my whisper of disbelief. "OhmyGod."

Charles's face is swollen, with hues of black and blue marring his face and blood veining the white of his eye. A cut on his top lip. He looks like he was attacked.

Turning to Valen, the question spills out, "What happened?"

Valen responds with a rapacious smile. "He slipped in the shower when he was bending over."

Charles's eyes dance between me and Valen nervously. Then to Garret. The two guys seated across and back to me.

"It happens," Charles explains, "when the tiles are wet. I slipped and—"

"Landed on your face and busted your lip at the same time," I interrupt, not believing it.

Valen grins. "He likes cock, Melody." He turns to Charles. "Isn't that right, Charles?" he muses. "You weren't thinking when you got hot and heavy with your boy toy."

"You're gay?" I ask Charles.

Charles shakes his head in a silent plea and winces when he remembers his face is all banged up. "No," he says solemnly.

"Yesterday, he was," Valen says with a dark resonance.

"You were there?" I ask with a flicker of curiosity.

Is Valen bi?

"No, but you heard what he said. The tiles were wet, so..." He pauses for a moment. "Let's go."

Panic sweeps over me when he stands, his movements fluid and deliberate as he swings his leg over the bench.

"That's okay. You can give me the assignment, and I'll be on my way," I suggest in a feeble attempt at control.

He draws near, his voice low and seductive. "Now, what would be the fun in that?"

The tiny hairs on my body stand. The air around us thickens, leaving his scent. My heartbeat syncs to an unknown rhythm.

Words fail me. My mind tries to scramble for a response, but I come up empty. No, yes. Fuck off. I don't want to go anywhere with you.

Fear and excitement amalgamated in my veins. If I say the last part, he will know the truth.

I'm afraid of him.

That he affects me.

I can't make sense of what I feel, but I'm attracted to him.

I lick my lips nervously, regretting choosing tights with a black skirt to wear this morning. They cling too tightly, not allowing the heat between my thighs to cool. It feels like I have a furnace between my legs when Valen is near me—intense and unyielding.

His gaze intensifies, the blue in his eyes dissolving into a stormy gray. "What do you want to eat?"

I want the ground to swallow me. His smile widens, fully aware of the turmoil he's causing, sending a flush of heat that seems to ignite every nerve ending, the sensation centering with an almost unbearable intensity of heat spreading around my clit like gasoline in a fire.

"I have plenty of places in mind," he says, "not too far, not too close." He steps forward, the chain dangling from his jeans with every stride. I find myself looking up, craning to meet his gaze, feeling dwarfed by his height. His eyes roam down my frame like he's measuring, assessing my size and how it compares to his.

"Where do you have in mind?" The words escape me, betraying me.

I can't believe I said that. I'm encouraging whatever he is trying to do. But this time, I'm different. I don't fall for fairy-tale bullshit or sexy smirks promising forever.

"Let's go," he says, turning around.

Casting a glance back at the table, I catch Charles's worried expression, which does nothing to ease my nerves.

I follow Valen, noting that he ignores all the appreciative glances from the girls who pass by. The head nods from the guys who know him. He's like a god walking across campus. I also don't miss the glances everyone gives me when they notice me following Valen to the parking lot. Like it's normal for a freshman to follow the most popular guy on campus. It's like they know something I don't. A huge secret I'm not privy to.

The lights flash from a blacked-out Porsche. He walks to the passenger side, opens the door, and gestures for me to get in with the palm of his hand.

I cross my arms over my waist.

"I'm not going to bite, Melody." His grin reveals a hint of darkness that sends a shiver down my spine. "Unless you want me to." I freeze, and he laughs. "I'm kidding." I step close to get in but pause when he leans in and says, "You should have seen your face. It looked like that is exactly what you needed."

"And what is that?" I say defiantly.

His nose barely inches from my ear, his breath a warm caress on the skin beneath my hair. A shiver mixed with heat and a pulse of desire that contradicts my rational mind slices through me.

"For me to remind you that you still exist, you can still bleed."

"You're crazy."

As I slide into the passenger seat, he pulls back, a shadow of amusement flickering in his eyes. "So I have been told." And he closes the door with a definitive thud.

We walk into an upscale steak and seafood restaurant on the outskirts of a designer strip mall called Legion. The server walks up, and he orders me a glass of white wine and himself a glass of water. I'm about to tell him I'm underage, but he winks at me and orders two lobsters.

When the server leaves, he smiles. "It's our little secret."

"What if I don't drink wine?"

My rebellious days are over, but I have. When I was fifteen, I tried every bottle of alcohol stashed in the house. Wine, liquor, and beer. I wanted to know what I liked so I wouldn't look like a prude when a guy asked me out to a party. Now, I stay away from anything involving alcohol. I know we're in a restaurant, and I don't think they drug their customers to fuck them in the back.

"What do you drink?"

"I drink what tastes good."

"You'll like what I ordered you."

"Don't get so cocky. I might not like what you give me," I shot back.

"You would have to try it first."

"I think I'm full."

"Satiety is ephemeral."

I lean back, trying to cool my inner turmoil. He's intense.

I take in the opulence of the restaurant. The restaurant adorns each table with pristine white tablecloths, the soft glow of faux candles flickering in their centers against the contrast of elegant black cloth napkins.

An array of blown glass fixtures crowns the bar above, their intricate designs casting a kaleidoscope of light across the polished surfaces. The waitstaff, in their crisp white shirts and black slacks, move with a practiced grace. The men in tailored suits, their conversations low and self-assured; the women in designer dresses, diamonds sparkling at their ears with every tilt of their heads. The air is thick with the scent of gourmet cuisine and the subtle undercurrent of affluence.

For me, this level of sophistication is uncharted territory. My parents considered a night out at Outback or Olive Garden the pinnacle of dining—places where our birthdays and graduations were celebrated, where family stories filled the air. Except for my graduation. I didn't get a graduation dinner. I was too busy finding a place to live when I left three weeks before graduation.

"What's on your mind?" he inquires, his gaze piercing as if he's trying to unravel the threads of my thoughts.

"I'm thinking this place seems...extravagant to just give me my assignment."

"You don't like it?"

"I didn't say that. It's more than I'm accustomed to."

"Have you ever been to a place like this?"

"Honestly, no. Your car costs as much as the house I grew up in."

He looks at me beneath his lashes. "Are you always this judgmental?"

"Do you always beat up your friends?" I blurt.

His eyes flash in amusement. He likes that I know he kicked Charles's ass.

"You caught that?"

"I did."

As our drinks arrive, he leans closer, the space between us charged with an unspoken tension. "And do you understand why, Melody?" He taps his finger on his temple, inviting me to delve deeper while he stares at me. "Think about it for a second. You're a smart girl. You can read me."

Can I?

"I've made you cathartic."

His teeth scrape his lips. "You're so hot. So, so close."

Jesus.

It's so hard not to think about sex when you're around him. He's like a walking sex object you want to stick up your pussy. Every word he utters has a double meaning, or he wants me to think it does. He could be playing around, but why me? He could fuck whoever he wanted. There is not a living, breathing female on campus who wouldn't fuck him. It's written over their faces when girls look at him. Hunger. Hope.

I know why he fucked up Charles. He fucked him up because of what he said. Because he made me uncomfortable.

"He said something that made me uncomfortable. He said he knows I like—"

His mouth rises. "Dick. He imagined you taking one."

"You're going to beat up everyone who says I'm taking one?"

He leans slightly over the table. "Is that what you want?"

"No."

I'm confused. Did he mean if I imagined his dick or any dick? I have to read between the lines. Everything he says has a purpose. Strategic. Like a maze, you have to figure it out.

"You imagine yourself taking cock, Melody? Is that too dirty for you?"

"What are you, my big brother?"

"No. You already have one of those."

"Are you asking me if I want to fuck, Valen?"

"Do you want to fuck, Melody?"

"Do you, Valen?"

I can play his game. I've been fucked over by worse assholes.

"I live and breathe to fuck. It's engraved in my soul."

"Then you don't need me. You have plenty of girls around to fuck with."

"What if I want to fuck you?" He leans closer to the table and lowers his voice. "Will you let me?"

"No," I say. "I have no interest in letting you fuck me, Valen."

He flinches like I slapped him. He's used to women opening their legs like a free ticket to a ride because of who he is and how hot he looks.

"How come?"

"I'm not your type."

I'm no one's type, but I don't need to explain myself to him.

"How do you know what my type is?"

"Blond, beautiful, with curves in all the right places." He

pinches his brows, and I continue, "I'm none of those things, and I'm not Jess."

His nostrils flare.

I hit a nerve. The one he thought I didn't know existed. Ears were made to listen, and I've heard that he fucked her. How he felt about her. She is all the things I mentioned he likes and more. She married his best friend. She made her choice. He probably carries a torch for her.

I'm the opposite of what she looks like. I'm fucked up, and the faster I get away from Valen, the better my chances are of saving myself.

I get up and drop the napkin on my table. Not caring, I almost spill the untouched glass of wine. I was never going to drink it anyway. I don't drink around men. I learned my lesson and paid handsomely for my mistakes.

"Where are you going?"

"I'm leaving." I lean in, my voice low but firm. "And a word of advice—whatever game you think you're playing, count me out. I'm sure plenty of girls will take you up on the offer."

I expected him to be surprised and shocked, but he isn't. He stares at me with a promise.

A silent vow that this isn't over.

CHAPTER SEVEN

VALEN

I WATCH the way her hips sway when she walks away. The way the globes of her ass lift with each step she takes in her short skirt. I came on too strong. I shouldn't have been so direct, but I couldn't help myself.

I want to fuck her. She doesn't know her brother sent her to a school full of predators. He thinks convincing me to grant her a scholarship is based on his being part of the outer ranks of the consortium. He thinks it grants her immunity. He doesn't realize you have to be born into one of the founding families or promise to be a member of the Order. He thinks she is safe here.

Melody Price is Prey, and everyone in Kenyan can see it. They smell it.

My cock screams for me to do whatever it takes for her to let me split her pussy and take what I want.

My balls ache, needing release. I stare at the glass of wine. The one she didn't drink.

Bringing her here was a test. She didn't touch the expensive wine. Another girl wouldn't have thought twice about a place like this or left before eating the two-hundred-dollar lobster I ordered. I was trying to showboat, and I failed miserably.

Melody Price cannot be bought with fancy dinners or expensive cars. She also can't be bought with promises of love and devotion.

Someone broke her, and it wasn't because her ex-boyfriend kicked her out of college the second she set foot on campus. I recognize that look on her face. The one she's hiding under the mask, but from what, or more importantly, from who?

I was surprised when she mentioned Jess. I would have never guessed she knew of my past or how I erroneously thought I was in love. Caring for and loving someone are two different things. I don't have the capacity to love when all I think about is my next pussy fix.

It's like snorting a line of coke and chasing a white horse that seems like a mythical creature of satisfaction. There for a moment, and then gone the next.

I don't know why I have this thing for Melody. When I first saw her at a party my sophomore year, trying to beat up her cheating boyfriend, I was amused. I wanted to kick his ass, but I wanted her more. I was filled with guilt because she was sixteen. I shouldn't want a girl that young.

When our eyes met for the first time, I didn't miss the way her eyes begged for the same thing that was going through my mind. She didn't love that asshole. I knew it. She knew it.

The second time I saw her was at a party a few months ago. She didn't see me, and at the time, I was on edge. I didn't like where my mind went, knowing she was so close. She was barely eighteen, and I didn't trust myself.

I left with Rachel and took it out on her at the closest motel. She didn't mind. I've been fucking my way through college, feeding my addiction. It's no secret, but I had no business having these thoughts for a girl fresh out of high school.

I could see it in her eyes. Melody wants the feeling of euphoria she thought her little boyfriend could give her. She knew, from the way I looked at her, that she didn't have a clue what it really felt like to break apart repeatedly. Hard. Rough. Pain. Pleasure.

I was angry when she left the table on campus. Her eyes no longer hold the fire they once did, which is the source of my concupiscence.

The server comes with our plates of lobster.

"Sir," the server asks with her brows raised, glancing at the seat in front of me like Melody is going to pop out from under the table.

"Please have her plate delivered with two cans of soda and a bottle of water," I instruct. "Make sure the lobster is warm with fresh bread. Also, include a message along with a wineglass." I hand her my black card. "Charge it to my card."

"What would you like to have it say once it's delivered?" she says, handing me a pen and paper.

I write on it and hand it to her. She doesn't look at it. At least not in front of me.

The chef rushes out nervously. A line of sweat drips from his forehead.

"Mr. Vikiar, was there something wrong with the lobster?"

"Everything was fine, Gerald. My lunch guest had an emergency. It's why I'm having it delivered. Please send a female courier."

He bows. "Of course, sir."

I look up, and the chef I hired from Italy gives me his full attention. "Don't be late. The hardware store closes at eight. I want her dinner there at six; no exceptions."

"Of course, sir."

By the time I walk out of my restaurant, she is already gone. Not how I planned things to go. The hostess indicated she took an Uber.

"Valen?"

I turn. Hate almost blinds my vision when Melissa walks up with Rachel. Her flavor of the week. Also, the same girl I fucked the night at the party, trying to forget the one I was thinking about.

"Melissa," I say in a tight voice.

She smiles with her red-painted lips, which does nothing for my cock. My balls dry up like prunes.

"I thought it was you." She turns toward Rachel. "This is Rachel. Rachel, this is my fiancé, Valen."

I grind my teeth. Melissa knows I fucked her. It's not like I hide it, but she likes to make a point.

"I'm not whatever she says I am."

Melissa gives me a tense smile. "It's our senior year, Valen. We both know what happens before we graduate."

"I get to continue fucking all of your friends."

Rachel gives me a once-over like I'm a porterhouse steak she wants to take a bite out of. Again. She doesn't like fish all that much. Too bad she poisoned herself with Melissa's smell.

"Hi, Valen. It's good to see you again," she says demurely. "We should hang out again sometime. Melissa talks so much about you."

"Does she?"

"All the time. She always reminds me how lucky she is."

"Well... I wouldn't call it lucky. More like... out of luck."

Melissa glances between Rachel and me. Anger flashes across her features at Rachel's flirting. Normally, I would let her think I'm going to fuck her and her friend but end up fucking her friend in the ass while Melissa eats her pussy, and then, when I'm done, come all over her face.

I haven't fucked her. I haven't since high school, and I never will. Especially after what she did to Jess.

Melissa is bi, but I think she's more of a lesbian. She wants me to hide it from her father, or he will disown her if I don't marry her.

Melissa has claws. Sharp ones. She will destroy everyone who thinks they have a chance with me.

She likes that I have a sex addiction because she doesn't have to worry about me falling in love with someone and voiding the whole arranged marriage stipulation our parents made when we were younger, per the rules of the Order.

"Why do you have to open your mouth?" Melissa says in a menacing tone.

"The same way you do... to get what I want."

"And what is that?"

Melissa gives me a once-over, not hiding the fact that I'm her exception to her every rule when it comes to sex.

"To avoid you. Like right now."

She smiles, but I can tell by the way she blinks that my words cut deep. The way her breathing turns shallow from the blow.

"Who do you want to fuck?" she asks, glancing at Rachel.

She thinks I want Rachel, and she is so pathetic that she would let me just to satisfy me.

"Not you." I glance at Rachel. "And not her."

Rachel's face falls. Melissa's eyes narrow. She senses something is up. She knows it's not in my character to turn down fresh pussy.

"Switching teams," she says, fishing for the truth.

"Enjoy yourself, Melissa. I'm sure Daddy would approve," I say, my words laced with a hint of irony. As I turn to walk away, I catch a glimpse of the storm brewing in her eyes.

Hate for what she can't have.

Melissa wants me, and she compensates by fucking women. She will do anything if it means she gets to keep me.

Too bad I have other ideas.

SWIM SEASON IS UNDERWAY. I'm at the very top of my game. My lap time in freestyle swimming is better every time I hit the water.

I pull myself out of the pool and catch Charles's gaze. "How's the face?"

He looks around and sees all the guys standing around with smirks on their faces. They know not to get involved.

"It hurts," he admits.

"That's a preview. Talk about her like that again, and I'll make sure the other side matches the right."

Charles comes from a family of wannabes. His father has money like most of the assholes in the Order, and was allowed in. He's not born into it.

"What is with you and this girl?" Garret asks.

I give him a glare. He nods, a silent acknowledgment that misses the mark. He assumes it's because she's just another Prey in my eyes. But it's more convoluted than that.

Garret is the last of his generation and treads lightly around me. He's acutely aware of the tension that simmers beneath the surface, a tension rooted in his past actions with Melissa and Jess. He said he didn't have a choice. He apologized. Veronica vouches for him, but he isn't a saint. He isn't a monk. Like all the rich kids sent here by their families, he enjoys getting his dick wet.

I didn't miss the way Charles was eye-fucking Melody, and I thought he was funny. I wanted to kill him. I thought of so many ways after she left. I kept staring at him with a murderous rage. I liked watching him squirm. I didn't like the way he said *dick* in front of her. He was picturing her in his mind. The way he gazed at her sent a direct message to his cock, causing his brain to shut down and any sense of morality to evaporate. When he is in that state, there is only one thing that pops into his brain: to fuck.

The first thrust and the last one are what take you over the edge. It disturbed me in ways I never dreamed of. The sensation of his hands on her skin was akin to a burning sensation, and I desired to evoke the same sensation in him. If I killed him, she would know, and I didn't want to scare her. Yet.

So I settled for the locker room shower, bashed his fucking face in, and sent a message. Don't think about touching her, and what would I do if a man uttered the word dick and her name in the same sentence.

"I-I'm sorry," Charles stammers. "I didn't know how you felt about her, man."

I grab a towel and dry off, heading to the locker room. "How do I feel, Charles?"

He walks behind me. "I don't know...um...you like her...more than like her. Obviously, we are protective of her."

I want to burst out laughing. He's afraid to say that I want to fuck her and get his skull crushed. I think he knows that I would kill him and have him buried in the cemetery on campus.

Garret walks in and looks worriedly in my direction. He's afraid of me these days. He thought Alaric and the Bedford twins, or even Reid, were psychotic. I'm in a whole different class of fucked up. He's never seen me fuck someone up for a girl I haven't stuck my dick in before. It's new. To anyone, that doesn't make sense. A sex addict who is protective over a girl he hasn't fucked. A girl he doesn't really know.

"Are you going to the frat party tonight?" Garret asks, changing the subject.

Charles, James, and Spencer look up with keen interest. They want pussy, and they know I'm the guy who could take them to the Promised Land.

"I'll meet up with you guys there."

Garret raises a brow. "I thought we would ride out together?"

"Ride with Charles. He has a blind spot on the side of his face."

Spencer laughs, and the whole locker room joins in. The right side of Charles's face turns red, and he looks funny.

CHAPTER EIGHT

MELODY

AFTER ENJOYING the most delicious lobster, Valen sent it with a note inside that read,

I want to feed you so you will never feel hungry. Fill you so you will never feel empty. I want to live inside you and hear you beg me for more.

V

I couldn't resist when I opened the container. The smell was heaven. I was ravenous and shamelessly horny, thinking about what he wrote. The chef had created a menu and a form where I could list my favorite meals, allergies, and the types of food I disliked. I filled it out and handed it to the older lady who delivered the food.

Ariel raised his brows in surprise when he saw the name of the restaurant printed on the bag. He asked if I was seeing anyone in Kenyan. I said no, but he wasn't convinced. He looked nervous but went back to work. I thought it strange but didn't trust him enough to ask.

After my shift, I walk to my car. My phone dings with an incoming text.

Valen: Look to the right.

Awareness prickles my spine, knowing he is here. I look to my right, and there is a blacked-out SUV with pitch-black tinted windows parked near the brush of trees. My phone dings again.

Valen: Get in.

Melody: So you can kill me?

He thinks I'm a stupid freshman who is going to fall for his crap.

Valen: If I wanted you dead, you would be.
Get in, Melody.

Fear curls in my stomach, but he's right.
I hesitate.
I look at my car and then at the black SUV. He bought me dinner. He said creepy shit with a double meaning, but for the most part, he hasn't been a total dick. He beat up a guy for saying I liked dick. It's a little over the top and a little red flag, but my brother said he would look out for me. I don't think Adam would allow me to be around a guy who would kill me.

A tense click resonates from my throat as I swallow hard, my steps automatic as they draw me across the cool pavement toward the SUV. The night comes alive with the chorus of crickets, their song intensifying with each step I take. The hum of the engine and then the fan when it clicks on those sounds like a breathing dragon.

The back passenger door swings open, spilling a soft, inviting light across the darkened ground. Hesitantly, I peer into the cavernous luxury of the car's interior, the rich scent of leather and a familiar woodsy cologne enveloping me, pulling me into its embrace. I slide into the plush captain's chair, my movements hesitant, only to meet the steady gaze of hazel eyes that hold a patience I can't fathom.

"I'm not going to hurt you, Melody," he assures, his voice a deliberate calm in the storm of my mounting anxiety.

"Then what are you planning to do?"

Everything happens fast. The back passenger door slams shut. The door locks, the driver slides in, and the car lurches forward.

"I need your help," he begins, the words catching me off guard. "I'm taking you somewhere to gauge your reaction. An experiment for my therapy."

"Therapy?" My voice echoes my confusion, the word hanging between us.

I wouldn't be surprised if he saw a shrink. He's a bit unhinged. Not normal by any means, but Zack and his friends weren't either. They didn't come with a warning label. At least with Valen, he gives you a hint.

"Yes," he confirms, his voice steady. "I want to see how you respond and what you think.

"Why would you care what I think?"

Where is he taking me, and why?

"Because... I don't know you the way I want, and you don't know me the way you wish you did."

"I..." I begin, hesitant, grappling with my thoughts. "I'm too young for you. I'm a freshman, and you're a senior."

"You're an adult, Melody. Legal, and will be turning nineteen in a month. I'm twenty-two. We are not that far apart in age."

"How do you know my birthday?"

But I do know. I think...

"Because you are in an Ivy League school because of me. Who did you think approved your scholarship?"

"My brother..."

"Doesn't know who did. He thinks what I want him to think. He made a request, and I honored it."

"Why?"

A moment of pause lingers. My palms sweat. I'm here because of him. He holds all the power with my future in his hands.

"I don't have to turn in the missing assignment, do I?"

He chuckles. The sound vibrates through me like a tug on a

guitar string. This is not about the assignment. He wouldn't go through all this trouble.

"You can turn it in if you want. It doesn't take too much time to complete. One is to write about a summer, and the other is a creative essay on anything you want to write about. I want to see it before you turn it in, though. If you decide you want to do it."

I take in his charcoal-colored jeans and black shirt with holes. I think they are supposed to be there. It's ripped on purpose. Everything he does is deliberate. Calculated.

"Why did you help get me into Kenyan?"

"Because I can, and I wanted to."

"You can do whatever you want."

He nods slowly. "For the most part, yes."

I watch the play of shadows over my hands, a distraction from the escalating tension. Suddenly, the interior light snaps on, and he hands me a bag. Inside, I find a cute cropped top, a perfect complement to my skirt and tights, and, notably, in my exact size. My gaze flickers to the driver, then back to him.

"Pull over." His eyes lock onto mine, unyielding. The car stops on the side of the road. "Get out." The driver gets out and shuts the door. "He's gone."

"But you're still here."

He closes his eyes.

A smirk plays at the corner of my lips. "You'll just open them the moment my shirt comes off."

"I won't," he vows, and the steadfastness in his tone almost convinces me. Almost.

"How can I trust you?"

"Trust is not earned, Melody. You have my trust, and I have yours. It's what we do to lose that trust—the actions that shatter it. Change."

"If that's the case, then why did you tell the driver to step outside?"

"You don't want to see what happens if he breaks my trust, Melody," he says with his eyes closed. "It will be bloody."

"You would kill him?"

"If he sees you change your shirt without my consent, I'll kill him. I don't think you want to see that. I want you to trust me. It's safe for you to change."

I look around. I wave my hand in front of his face, but he doesn't move. He doesn't flinch. His eyes are closed. The only light is from the dim light coming from the floorboard and the strip of light on the door panels.

I take a second to admire how beautiful he is. My eyes trail over his ripped arms, memorizing the tattoos of skulls and crows. My eyes find the piercing on his lip. The glint of the small diamond piercing his nose. His lashes are long and dark despite his blond hair.

I pull the polo shirt over my head. I can see the grin playing on his lips. I lean close to check if he's trying to steal a glance.

"Are you wearing a bra?"

I grab the black cropped top from the bag. "Yes."

"Color?"

"Black."

I pull the shirt over my head. Over the swell of my breasts. The fabric is soft and tight. It's comfortable and smells like a boutique store.

He sticks his hand out. "Give me your hand."

His eyes close when I lean over and slide the palm of my hand into his. His hand is large, warm, and strong. The smell of his cologne makes me dizzy. I reach out to steady myself.

My eyes pop open. I was too busy admiring the feel of his hand, not realizing I was touching the crotch of his jeans. His cock is hard.

"Valen," I whisper.

"I don't have to see you to know that I want you, Melody. The thought of you in a bra with my eyes closed is enough." I snatch my hand back. "Is it safe for me to open my eyes?"

He didn't see me. If he did, I'm sure he wouldn't feel the same way.

"Yes."

I look out the window. His driver leans with his back against the car, scrolling through his phone. Valen taps the window, signaling that it's safe to come inside.

We arrive at a frat party. The last place I would agree to go, but for some reason, walking in with Valen has me at ease. Maybe it's because he could have taken advantage of me inside the car, but he didn't, or because I'm attracted to him.

He doesn't stop to chat and ignores everyone trying to get his attention. One of the girls, sipping a beer in the corner, directs a seductive smile at him. Some I've seen walking around campus. Some are from my class, and others I have never seen before.

He heads down a hallway, opens a door, and steps aside to let me through.

"Why are we here?"

"So I can show you something," he says.

Panic sets in when I see a bed. I whirl around, but he blocks me. "That is not for you. I didn't bring you here to do something you wouldn't want to do. I'll explain."

"Explain what?" I say harshly. "I didn't agree to this."

"I get that, but I want you to understand me."

"What? You're a creep."

He smiles and pushes me against the wall.

My eyes go wide. It's dark. "Please," I plead.

I don't know what I'm asking. I don't want to walk out of here without him in the crowd of people. I also don't want to be alone here.

I close my eyes. "Melody."

"Yes," I whimper.

"Are you wet?"

I nod. Fuck. What is wrong with my body? When I'm around him, I can't think straight.

The sound of a door opening has my eyes snapping open. Two girls and a guy walk in.

They spot Valen, and then they glance at me.

The blonde smiles in my direction. "She can join if she wants."

"She's here for me," Valen says in a curt tone.

The brunette next to her pouts. "Oh, that's too bad."

The guy looks away when he spots Valen shielding me from his gaze.

Are they going to fuck? The guy kneels on the bed while both women undress. The man takes off his clothes. He is muscular and good-looking. He's not old. None of them are. They look around the same age as Valen, but I don't recognize them from school.

The brunette starts sucking the guy's cock while the blonde eats her ass. They both moan, and it's hot. It's like watching live porn.

Valen stands behind me, and I can feel his erection on my lower back. Jealousy rises like a rash over my skin, wanting him to be hard because of me, and I hate myself for it. I'm so messed up. How can I feel this way after what happened?

His breath fans my ear, and he whispers, "I have a sex addiction, Melody. I'm addicted to pussy," he admits. "I like to watch and fuck. It's my high. My fix. My need." He grinds his cock on me.

He pulls my hair over one shoulder. The cool air kisses my skin. His breath warms it back up. I'm about to catch fire. My nipples ache, my pussy drips, and I want his cock to be where the blonde has her tongue—in my cunt. I want him to fuck me, but I can't. I'm afraid to experience sex again.

The brunette continues to suck the guy's cock and dips her tongue into his balls. The blonde slides her fingers into the brunette's cunt and continues to tongue her ass. The brunette hums on the guy's balls, and he grunts with pleasure. As he pulls her hair and thrusts his cock deep into her throat, she gags. Saliva drips down her chin. He fucks her mouth, and she moans.

He pulls out and comes on the brunette's face. Her tongue is out, lapping it up, and I'm hot and wet.

I shamelessly push back against Valen's erection. His mouth is near my ear, and his hands hold me steady at my waist.

"Do you like it? Do you like feeling me hard while you get wet watching them fuck?"

"Yes."

"You want me to do that to you, don't you, Melody? Since the day we first laid eyes on each other."

There's a whimper, and it's coming from my mouth. "Um..."

I can't think.

The brunette opens her mouth, cum dripping on her face. She lets out a moan as she orgasms from the blonde sucking her cunt.

"Tell me," he says, "you wanted me to suck your cunt when you first saw me. Tell me the truth, Melody. I remember the look in your eye, but we couldn't. I wanted you, but I couldn't touch you. I couldn't ask you what you wanted. I had to... forget you." He pushes his dick against my ass over my skirt. "I thought I could ask. I thought I could, but it wasn't right." His body trembles behind me like he's holding back. "But now I can." His lips brush over my skin. "Show me how wet your pussy is for me. How much it needs to be filled. Fight whatever it is that holds you back."

"Who are they?"

The blonde pulls away from the brunette's pussy and licks the cum off the brunette's face, then sucks the guy's dick.

"Rich college kids that like to share." I slide my hand between my legs, and I'm soaked. "Let me see."

I hold up my hand, my fingers glistening from my arousal. He slides his tongue between my fingers and sucks. A wave of pleasure shoots straight to my clit as I watch him close his eyes, savoring the taste. The feel of his soft tongue over my fingers. It's a drug for him. The way his breathing silently gives him away at how much he enjoys the taste of me thrills me.

I look over my shoulder, and the two girls are getting dressed. Their fuck session is over.

"Valen, they are leaving."

His eyes open, and he smiles. "So are we."

Relieved that we aren't staying, I follow him down the hallway to a side door that leads outside to the awaiting SUV.

CHAPTER NINE

VALEN

WE SIT in the back of the car on the long bench. She's behind the driver's chair, and I'm sitting in the center. I don't want to tempt the driver into looking at the rearview mirror when she is wearing a skirt.

She doesn't realize how beautiful her body is. How perfect her ass looks or how high her breasts sit in the top I bought her. She doesn't think she's beautiful.

The way she mentioned Jess told me all I needed to know. Melody doesn't think she is attractive, but she is also jealous of the thought of me with someone else. I could see it in her eyes when she mentioned her. I felt it when she thought my cock wasn't hard for her.

"Why are we sitting back here?" she asks.

I stretch my legs out and lean close. "Because you're wearing a skirt, baby. I don't want anyone to imagine what you look like between your legs."

She glances at the driver. "Just you?"

"Only me."

"How presumptuous of you."

"You'll get used to it."

She scoffs. "Who do you think you are?"

I lean closer and reply softly, "The one you think about when you play with your pussy. I'm the man you fantasize about when you imagine yourself to be a whore. I'm the man who has libidinous thoughts about you."

"You're crazy."

"Am I? All women do it. The virgins. The moral wives of men

while their husbands are philandering behind their backs. All women wonder what it would be like if they weren't judged so harshly for liking sex the same way men do."

"But you have a problem," she whispers.

"You mean my satyriasis."

I find it amusing that she thinks people don't know—like my driver. He's been driving me around since I was twelve. He's seen my bare ass pump inside countless women.

"Don't worry, Melody. I'm not going to fuck you if that's what you're worried about. I'm not going to do anything you don't want."

"Why?"

My lips skirt the edge of her shirt right above her left breast, watching her nipples go as hard as rocks. I love working her up. I want her to feel how beautifully her body responds to me. I get off on it.

"Because I need your consent."

"To what?" she asks, confused.

"To fuck you, Melody. I need your consent to fuck you like you want me to. I want you to smile when you see me naked between your legs. Your screams when I send you over the edge, and your vision blurs with how hard I pound into your tight cunt, but I don't want to take if you don't want me to."

She leans over my legs, and my cock hardens painfully inside my jeans. Fuck, fuck, fuck. I want to fuck her so bad, but I can't.

Her eyes fall to the piercing on my lip. The one she looks at like a snack she wants to try. I flick my tongue over it. My cock is wet. My balls ache. Desire runs like fire inside my veins. My fingers clench my thighs.

"Melody," I whisper.

She looks between my legs. It's dark, but she can tell by my voice that I'm on the edge. My eyes almost roll to the back of my head. I love her hair. It's a different shade than my own, and I like how soft and shiny it looks. I want to feel the tips on my skin while she rides me.

"I don't want to fuck you, Valen." Her words stab me in the chest. "I don't want to have sex."

Is this how it feels to die?

She steps over my legs. Her ass brushing past my face.

She reaches for the door handle and then opens it. I look out the window, and we are at the hardware store.

The door slams shut, and I watch her run to her car. The driver knows to wait until she starts her car and safely drives off.

The piece of shit Mazda looks like it's fighting to breathe when it makes a noise after she places it in drive. The yellow lights glare past us like two flashlights when she turns on the road.

I place my cell phone over my ear. "Follow her."

My driver looks at me through the rearview mirror. "Where to, sir?"

"Home."

I want to follow her myself, but that would scare the shit out of her. She's resisting me, and it's something I'm not used to. It's refreshing but gutting me from the inside.

I can't think.

I can't breathe without having her near me.

I swipe my hand down my face. I'm losing my fucking mind. Porn doesn't do it for me anymore. I'm trying to hold back and not play with her head. She is the only woman who gives me the control I've wanted since I was a teenager and knew the feeling of what it was like to come. Since I've laid eyes on her now that she is an adult, all I can think about is her.

The SUV pulls through the gate of my father's estate. The darkness my father prefers is like a velvet cloak, smothering most of the light coming from the trees in the red spotlights.

The path to the house is a flickering dance of light and shadow, with fire torches lining the way, casting long, twisting shapes against the backdrop of ancient trees. At the heart of the driveway, a grand fire blazes like a beacon for some arcane ritual. My father has always been drawn to the flame, claiming it mirrors the fire within us all—that primal force fueled by desire and disdain, capable of making our blood sing with heat. And now, as I think of Melody, I understand those words with a clarity that pierces through the darkness. My desire for her is a relentless flame, an insatiable fire that courses through me, demanding attention and action.

I walk inside and don't miss my father sitting in the huge wingback chair with two women sucking his cock. They both look up, their mouths glistening. Something I've gotten used to since my mother died.

My mother was the first Prey married into the Order. The love of my father's life. She died giving birth to my brother, which is a silent testament to the life my mother once carried. Disowned and disparaged, he's a living reminder of the loss that broke him. He is three years younger than me, and my father banished him because of his hatred. My father forbids him from leading a life of privilege and hates his existence. He blames my little brother for my mother's death, and no one can speak of him. It's like he's a bastard child with no rights. No luxuries. No college education. No money or chauffeurs.

My little brother exists because of me.

He eats because of me.

Through it all, my brother loves me. I'm god in his eyes. If he only knew, he is the best thing in my life, and I feel guilty that I can't do more.

"Did you come from seeing the maggot?" he says, his voice dripping in disdain as he adjusts his pants.

The women scurry out of the living room.

After my mother died, Vance Vikiar turned into a womanizer. His only love is in a grave. No one speaks about it. No one mentions it. Everyone acts like my parents are both alive and well. It couldn't be farther from the truth. My father taught me not to love a woman. He warned me that losing her would ruin me forever.

My father didn't set foot in a church after my mother died. Not a real one anyway. The church in Kenyan is not a real church. As the sun sets, evil unites, turning the cross upside down.

"No," I reply, sidestepping the question.

"Well, where were you?" He sneers, eyeing the deliberate tears in my shirt.

Another thing he hates. The way I dress.

"Are you out of money?"

"No, why?"

"Then why do you have holes in your shirt? Have you no shame?"

I want to laugh in his face. My shirt cost more than his shoes, but I see that he doesn't understand fashion. My father adheres to traditional values. He prefers suits and aged scotch. Gold instead of brass. I'm surprised he doesn't have a gold toilet to take a shit on.

"It's designer."

"It's pedestrian, Valen. Is that what women like nowadays? Men fucking them with holes in their shirts?"

From my recent experience, no. But I don't tell him that.

"I don't think women care what you're wearing when you fuck them."

"Don't be funny, Valen. How's Melissa?"

"I wouldn't know, and I don't care."

He chuckles behind me as I walk toward the kitchen.

"You know she doesn't care about your sexual proclivities. She's perfect for you, Valen."

"No, she isn't. If you think she's so perfect, why don't you marry her?"

He wouldn't because he isn't into young girls around my age. It's not his thing. He's against remarrying. Re-committing.

He leans on the counter, watching me make a cup of coffee. "You know how I feel about that, so don't test me. What is going on with you? You've been acting strange since last year. You don't partake in your usual fun."

He means orgies.

"I'm taking a break."

He laughs. "Who's the girl?" he asks quietly.

"There isn't a girl."

"You don't think I could tell when my son is lying?"

I shrug. "I wouldn't know. You have two sons."

He slams his fist on the counter. "I have one son," he yells, then straightens his shirt.

I hate reminding him of my younger brother, but I don't want him to know about Melody. No one can know, or she will become a target.

I have enough with guys trying to fuck with her on campus. I see the way they look at her, which invokes the demon inside.

She was forbidden then, and she's forbidden now. She was too young at the time, and I'm betrothed to a woman who would do anything to make her disappear if she found out how much I wanted her. Melody has no protection on campus. I can't make her want me. I can't claim her if she doesn't consent. Rules are rules.

I've already broken so many when it comes to her.

I pull out my phone when a text comes through. I see the pin on her location when she makes it home, and a picture.

Fuck!

CHAPTER TEN

MELODY

"LOOK AT HER. SHE WANTED IT."

I jolt awake, a strangled gasp tearing through the silence, a scream clawing its way up my throat, threatening to choke me. I cough, desperate for air, my hands frantically wiping at the imagined moisture on my neck. My fingertips come away damp—not from sweat but from the tears that have carved paths down my cheeks.

It was only a dream.

For the first three months, I had them every day. I was glad I wasn't in my room, or my parents would hear my screams.

I look around and see the rough plastic that makes the interior walls of the trailer. I scrubbed them the best I could the first day, but the yellow sheen still bleeds through.

It smells like grass and leaves from the small opening of the vent I left open to let the cool breeze in.

My throat is sore. I must have been screaming because it feels like I swallowed rocks.

I open the small fridge I bought on sale at Walmart for twenty-five bucks with the blue Pepsi logo on it. It doesn't hold much, but I don't have much.

I kneel and look out the small window to see if anyone is outside. I used to love scary movies and watched them whenever I was bored and home alone. Funny how you stop watching them when you live like you're in a set on one.

When I slept in my car, I imagined a serial killer dragging me out and mutilating me. When I slept in the trailer for the first time, I thought a man with a mask would come and get me with a butcher knife. The jitters set in, like the first night. I look left and right, and the branches sway, followed by the chirping of crickets. A coyote howls, probably because of the full moon.

I'm peering out the window for a minute or two when my phone rings. I look over at the bright screen lighting up. I reach over and answer, placing it on the speaker, then wait for my brother to speak.

"Hello, Melody?"

"I'm here."

"Hey."

"Hey."

Silence.

"Umm, how are you? How's school?"

Your rich friend wants to fuck me.

"It's good. Everyone is nice."

"Listen, um... I wanted to ask if you could come and watch me play on Friday. It's our first game, and I really want you to be there."

I sit and pull my knees up. "Um..."

"Mom and Dad can't go. They have this thing they have to go to for Dad's work, and I thought—"

I close my eyes. They will be there. I want to kick myself for telling Adam that the whole Zack thing was in the past. It was a stupid high school mistake. I left the house for this reason. So they wouldn't find me. At Kenyan, they would be too busy with practice and school to show up on campus. There's security. There is...Valen.

"Melody?"

"Yeah, yeah. I'm here."

"Will you go?"

My hands are sweating and shaking. All my saliva has dried up in my mouth. I feel hot and cold. My vision blurs, and I can hear my heart pounding. The beginning of a panic attack.

I started getting them after that night. I googled the symptoms after the third time they came around. I usually get them when I'm alone or when something triggers them. A sweaty odor from a locker room or a gym. The smell of spit or a man when he sweats. The dark.

I read there was medication doctors prescribed for it, but I can't go to the doctor. I don't have my insurance card, and it would mean I would have to ask my parents for it, which I refuse. I close my eyes, hoping it's a quick one this time.

"Melody, are you alright?"

"I'm fine," I say, blowing out a slow breath. "I'll go," I agree.

"Don't worry about a thing. I got you a ticket," he says. "I'll text it to you. It's going to be fun," he says with a smile in his voice. "And don't worry, no one on the team knows you'll be coming to see me. I really want you to be there."

He means Zack.

Zack will be there with the others. I need to stay hidden in the crowd. It shouldn't be too hard. I'll wear a black hoodie over my head and black pants.

"Okay."

"Thank you. It means a lot to me that you're there for my first game."

After we say goodbye, I sit in the same spot on the sleeping bag after a cold shower. My hair is wet, cooling my flushed skin. I close my eyes, willing sleep to come. I try to think of anything but that night. It comes in and out. Like the air from my lungs. In and out, in and out. Just like my memories. It arrives in fragments. I don't want to make out each voice, but I know I have to at some point.

They took turns.

It was five or six, maybe. I could have sworn I heard a female voice, but it could have been the drugs they slipped into my drink that night that distorted my hearing and vision. I blacked out at some point from the pain between my legs, and then everything went numb. It felt like I was on a rower, sliding up and down.

It felt wet, hot, and then cold. The smell of sweat and their sex. Musk. I heard a few names, maybe three. My head was fuzzy. Jacob, Sam, and Zack.

After it was over, I became a college statistic. The victim in a horror story is a girl attending a college party. Guys who drug a girl to take advantage of her.

But you let those things slide because you think there's no way it can happen to you.

You graduated from high school. You're an adult. You're fearless. You have a big brother who goes to the same school. A sister who accepts and loves her sexuality and isn't afraid to show the world that she is comfortable. You're smarter than they think you're capable of. You have overprotective parents, and you don't think it's fair that they don't let you go out late because they are trying to keep you safe. You start to resent them because there is a boy who smiles the right way and tells you the things you want to hear. You don't want to believe what they are capable of. What they can do when you don't give them what they want.

I had a stable home with perfect siblings, but I wasn't careful about exploring love, sex, and friendships. The guy I gave my virginity to absquatulated; he treated me like a cherry-pick, and I ended up being caught in a web of assholes who took advantage of me. Monsters of the worst kind. They ripped any notion I had about love and exploration of my sexuality from underneath my skin without a clear memory of how they did it.

I grab a pen and paper and begin to write.

Hopefully, I will have something to turn in tomorrow for class. It's a good thing there is nothing to distract me. I don't have a TV and need to charge my phone to wake up on time in the morning for class. I'm sure I'll be swamped with homework for the next three days. Valen said I didn't have to do it, but then the professor would know.

I don't want special treatment or for everyone to think I fucked Valen. It would mean Zack and his friends were right.

My thoughts go to the bedroom where he took me. The two girls and the guy having sex in the room while a party was going on outside. The way he was hard when he was standing behind me showed me the sexual exigency his body felt. The smell of his cologne. The way his lips ghosted my skin. I wanted him at that moment more than anything I have ever wanted, and it clouded my judgment.

I remember the movement in photographic detail. His breath on my neck tickled my ear. The eroticism of his touch. The need for him to taste me the same way. To be his, but I knew being his would mean I would have to share him.

The other part of me screamed in warning. I wasn't beautiful like those women he was hard for. I wasn't blond or pretty. I didn't wear makeup or have pretty tanned skin. I didn't have a body like theirs either. I didn't have confidence or self-esteem. Predators take what you can't easily get back. Your life. The ability to trust someone again. Your sexual prowess.

CHAPTER ELEVEN

VALEN

I'M SITTING in class next to the seat Melody was in on Monday. The guys sit on the same side, below me. They don't say anything when I don't sit with them because they know not to. They know I'm interested in her. But who isn't?

I'm interested in her in a different kind of way. I want to fuck her, but not just once. I want something real. I want to be around someone for once who doesn't look at me like I'm a sex-crazed freak who is only good for one thing. Sex and money. I want someone smart like me. A person who looks at things differently. I checked her school records. She was valedictorian, but what doesn't make sense is that she almost didn't graduate for missing school.

I watch people file in and take their seats. Girls I have slept with in the past give me a wink or a knowing smile that I don't return. I fix my gaze on the door, observing each individual as they walk by.

Adriana spots me and walks up the aisle. She's about to take the seat next to me when I announce, "This seat is taken." She looks up in surprise. "I'm waiting for someone."

"Come on, Valen," she says coyly. "We can get something to eat after."

Before Melody showed up, I would have taken her up on her offer, but I'm not interested. I'm hungry, but it's not for her.

I wave my hand, shooing her away, when the door opens and Melody walks in. She looks gorgeous in ripped black jeans, a cropped sweater, and black combat boots. Her hair falls around her shoulders like silk.

I ignore Adriana and gesture for Melody to sit next to me.

She looks at Adriana's stank face with uncertainty and resigns, taking the seat in front.

"Prey," Adriana says, softly shaking her head in disbelief.

My Prey.

I ignore Adriana, but she doesn't move. I look up, annoyed. "What?"

"She isn't interested in you, Valen. Be a good boy and take what's right in front of you."

"I'm not interested," I say in a flat tone.

"Aren't you too old for her?"

"Aren't you too old to act like you're in high school? Desperate for the popular guy to notice you."

Her face turns red, and she storms off, looking around, hoping no one heard me insult her. Adriana's father is in the Order, but a low-key member that helps export whatever the fuck we want in and out of where we see fit. She's a kleptomaniac. She steals for fun and only pays if she gets caught.

Professor Owens walks in, looks at the podium, and picks up a paper I didn't see there when I walked in.

"Miss Price," he calls, looking around the room.

She raises her hand. "I'm here," she says and lowers her hand.

"Would you read it to the class? It's part of the assignment."

I see her stiffen. She hesitates for a split second.

She remembered the assignment. I wonder what she wrote about one of her summers. I told her to let me see it before she turned it in, but she didn't.

She doesn't trust me.

I wonder what she did that I'm not privy to. I want to know what she likes. Her college applications said she aspires to be a writer, which is one of the reasons she is enrolled in this class.

She gets up and takes the paper. She goes back to her seat, making it a point not to look at me.

Her gaze sweeps the room. Everyone looks in her direction. She looks down at the paper and begins:

"For some, summer is warm. It can be a time when you fall in love. The nights are longer. When you're asked out by someone who says you're special, you look up at the dark sky, see the stars, and hope you can burn together and become one. You trust him because he said you could. He's my person in him. It's one of those moments you think is perfect. The kind that you replay in your mind before you fall asleep. The kind that gives you dimples on your skin from goose bumps. The kind that makes you feel liquescent, glistening under the stars.

But my last summer wasn't warm. It was cold. Wounds would turn into deep scars, bandaging my heart. He wasn't my person. He was a lie. There were no stars in the dark sky. No wishes to burn as one.

There was laughter. He expressed how he thought of me. How ugly I looked. How nasty I felt. I would do anything to fit in. Reminding me that everything I thought about love was a lie. My body was just currency for a sick, twisted game.

I looked up, not knowing what was happening all around me. All I remember is how my breathing stopped. How my hands shook when he laughed about the way I looked without my clothes. It was the summer I would never forget because I lost so much. You see, I was so desperate to live life and fall in love. I didn't know everything I wished for would be taken from me. My confidence. The spark behind my eyes when I looked in the mirror. The beauty I thought I possessed. The love I thought I had. I fell.

I fell into a dark hole, and now I'm here."

She puts the paper down. My hands are numb from how hard I'm gripping the edge of the table.

Silence stretches throughout the room.

Professor Owen clears his throat. "Thank you, Miss Price."

Garret glances at her and then at me. My eyes land on the back of her head, and I know after hearing about her summer, she won't turn around. How could she? Someone hurt her, and it wasn't just one asshole. There were more.

She couldn't breathe.

Her hands shook.

How ugly I looked.

How nasty I felt.

Who would laugh about how nasty someone felt? I'm trying to piece together what she read aloud in my head, searching for clues like shifting puzzle pieces. The pieces are trying to fit. To make sense of it.

How nasty I felt.

How ugly I looked.

Laughter.

Not, he laughed.

I think of Jess. Veronica. Different scenarios are all pleating together.

When?

How?

Time passes in a blur. I remain seated after everyone files out of the room, including Melody. She kept her head down the whole time, avoiding eye contact with me.

Garret walks up. "Hey, man. I..."

"I'll see you at practice. Watch her for me until I come back," I tell him.

He nods. "Alright, Valen."

"WHAT BRINGS you to my office today, Mr. Vikiar?" Dr. Wick inquires, her tone striving for professionalism yet carrying a hint of performative courtesy.

"I'm here because I need to talk, Dr. Wick. Isn't that the crux of your profession? To listen to those of us grappling with our minds, even when the solutions seem elusive."

I notice she's somewhat disheveled today, her usual attire replaced by less formal clothing, perhaps caught off guard by my unexpected visit. Her attempt to cross her legs discreetly in her pantyhose—a vain effort to conceal the varicose veins that betray her age—doesn't escape my attention.

"What seems to be the problem today?" she asks, adjusting to the shift in our usual dynamic.

I settle into my chair, stretching my legs, and without much thought, I light a joint and take a slow, deliberate drag. The smoke curls and dances under the fluorescent lights—a visual echo of my search for the right words.

She's stopped protesting. I'm over twenty-one. It's legal to smoke weed recreationally now in the state of Ohio, so there isn't much she can do about it.

"I've been experiencing certain episodes," I finally say, watching the smoke linger in the air.

"What type of episodes are you referring to?"

I hesitate, then admit, "Episodes filled with intense desire... lechery, lasciviousness."

"I see. Recognizing these patterns is crucial. Would you say these are fantasies driven by an underlying compulsion?"

"It's like hunger. The same way you feel the need to cheat on your husband with colleagues, Dr. Wick."

I like to remind her that she is no different from my '*Don Juanism*' when she's impulsive. She shifts uncomfortably in her seat. She is on the fence about me knowing about her little problem of promiscuity. She wants me to know because she imagines it is me that she fucks. I see the hungry glint in her eyes when she looks at my crotch. She is curious about the length of my cock. What color it is, girth, or if I'm circumcised.

"What are you hungry for? The chase? The high?"

My eyes flick to her, and I see her throat move as she swallows. "Prey."

Her nose flares. "I see."

"I want her."

"Is this the same girl?"

"Yes. She's here."

"How did you..."

"I brought her here."

"Why?'

"You know why?"

"Does she have any romantic feelings toward you, Valen? If this is purely physical..."

"No... I'm not sure, but I'm working on it. I don't know how to."

"What do you want with this girl besides the obvious?"

She knows I haven't fucked, or I wouldn't be here. She's my control, and it's slipping.

"I want her to like me. I want her to see me as her god. I want to own her. I want to fuck her everywhere."

"Do you pleasure yourself?"

I chuckle. "All the time, Dr. Wick. My cock has more ladders than a hardware store."

"To her."

"Five times this morning."

"Have you had sex with anyone else since she's been here?"

"No."

"I see."

"She doesn't want me."

She sits up in her chair. "This is a first for you."

I nod. "I can't think unless I have her, but I want her to want me and only me. She's my obsession."

"No other girl will do."

I shake my head. "I don't want another girl. I want her, Dr. Wick, and I'll do anything to have her, but I don't want to hurt her."

"You have to try, Valen. Meaningful relationships are hard for sex addicts. In your case, you have a strained relationship with your father because of your mother's death. The only thing you have learned when it comes to relationships with women is what your father has taught you." I grin, and she continues, "What do you plan to do with your fiancée?"

I burst out laughing. "Oh…Dr. Wick. You still think I'll be a good husband?"

"Why not? Your father thinks so, or he wouldn't have secured an alliance."

She thinks I would tell her my plans and incriminate myself to the Order. How clever.

I widen my smile. The one that makes her sweat.

"I don't plan to do anything with her yet."

"I see… What do you plan to do about this girl?"

"I want to go on a date," I say simply.

"Then ask."

"I tried, but…"

"She turned you down?" Her eyes light up with interest.

I lean back in my seat and look straight at her. "She did."

"Hmm… try harder… or maybe she doesn't like you."

"She does."

"How do you know?"

"I know," I say quietly.

"Change the narrative. Change what people say about you. Show her the person you want to be with her, Valen. Who do you want to be when she looks at you? The sex addict with a temper, or the perfect guy in her eyes."

"How?"

"Talk to your friends." She means to talk to Reid, Dravin, and Draven. I want to laugh and throw up. Imagine me writing love letters.

"Valen?"

I blink twice. "Yes?"

"If you want to show her and are really interested in this girl, find out what she likes without talking about sex. Learn to control your impulsivity. I think this will be good for you. I like this girl already."

"Because she turned me down?"

She uncrosses her legs and smiles. "Especially because she turned you down. Have you used drugs?"

"No."

She looks up, writing in my chart. "Last time?"

"Party about six months ago."

"The one where you were trying to forget…"

"Yes."

"You're a smart young man," she continues, "very smart. Genius even. I'm surprised you haven't graduated early." She pauses for a moment, like she just realized something. "You…"

"Waited," I finish for her.

"For her."

"I did," I admit. "I waited for her."

"Why?"

"It's what I'm trying to figure out."

CHAPTER TWELVE

MELODY

HE SENT me two tickets to see if I made a friend or had a boyfriend. I look up when I hear Ariel help a customer out the door.

He turns around, and our eyes meet. "Hey, Ariel?"

"Is everything okay?"

He's not used to people talking to him unless they need help around the store.

He sent me two tickets to see if I made a friend or had a boyfriend. I look up when I hear Ariel help a customer out the door.

He turns around, and our eyes meet. "Hey, Ariel?"

"Is everything okay?"

He's not used to people talking to him unless they need help around the store.

"Are you doing anything later?"

He shifts nervously on his feet. He blinks a couple of times. I don't think anyone has ever asked him to go anywhere. A girl even less with the way he is looking at me. Nervous and indecisive.

"No."

"My brother sent me two tickets to the Ohio football game, and I was wondering if you want to go with me."

He stuffs his hands in the pockets of his stonewashed jeans and looks at his dirty work boots. "You want to go with me?"

"Why not?"

He shrugs. "I thought you had a boyfriend. The one that sent you food."

I can understand why he would think that. Also, the car that waits for me after work.

Valen has a driver wait for me until I get home. I tried to ignore it and thought it would stop after a few days, but it hasn't. I also thought if I ignored him in class, he would get the hint that I wasn't interested.

"I don't have a boyfriend."

He looks up. "You're not seeing anyone?" He shakes his head. "I don't want any problems."

I give him a reassuring smile. "I'm not, and it's not a problem. I don't want to go alone, but if you don't want to go, I understand."

His eyes widen. "I do," he rushes out. "I'll go."

"Alright," I say with a smile.

After taking a shower, I meet Ariel back at the hardware store. I'm surprised when he pulls in the lot in a brand-new black raptor. It looks pricey and not something he could easily afford working at the hardware store. I didn't see it in the parking lot, or it must be new.

"Nice truck," I point out after closing the door.

His hand grips the steering wheel, looking out the windshield. "Thanks," he replies, his voice carrying a hint of pride and a small smile lifting the corners of his mouth.

There's a subtle scent that seems uniquely his, comforting and inviting. Casually dressed in blue jeans and a gray sweater, he has a flush to his cheeks, a rosy hue suggesting he was trying his best to fix his complexion.

To be honest, I'm not into football. I'm here for my brother—he's playing," I explain, hoping to make him feel more at ease with the situation.

"That makes sense," he responds, with a note of relief.

We fall into a brief silence, the kind that feels like it's waiting to be broken.

"So..." I begin, unsure of where to steer our conversation next.

"My name isn't actually Ariel," he admits.

"Oh?" Of all the things he could have said, this was the last I anticipated. "Why does everyone call you Ariel, then?" I ask, curiosity piqued.

He chuckles lightly. "Well, when I started working at the hardware store after school, Mr. Crosby had trouble pronouncing my real name. He started calling me Ariel instead, and it just stuck. I've been working there since I was fifteen, so after a while, I just got used to it," he explains.

"My real name is Azriel," he reveals.

"Azriel," I say, testing it out. The name rolls off my tongue with a sense of familiarity and identity that 'Ariel' never quite captured.

It is an unusual name. Mr. Crosby is an old timer, and it would make sense for him to have a bit of trouble pronouncing it. I like it.

"I like Azriel better."

"You do?"

"Actually, I prefer Azriel to Ariel. It suits you better."

He nods, with a hint of relief. "Outside the hardware store, everyone calls me Azriel. I just wanted you to know in case we bumped into someone I know. It might be confusing to hear them call me something different," he explains. "I've never really liked 'Ariel,' but Mr. Crosby has been like a mentor to me, so I never corrected him."

"Mr. Crosby is a stand-up guy. He helped me find a job and a place to live when I was in a tight spot," I share.

"How come?" he asks.

"It's a long story," I reply, my gaze drifting out the window mindlessly. "I had to leave my parents' house." No wanting to open the door that leads to too many questions. I ask, "Do you live with your parents?"

"No."

"Oh..."

"You go to Ohio?" He asks, obviously changing the subject.

"No... I...well... I used to and then transferred to Kenyan."

The car jerks slightly as he finds a parking spot, the mention of Kenyan drawing a surprised reaction. "Kenyan?

"Yeah."

"Wow. I-I mean, that's great, but how?"

"I got a scholarship."

"Oh, that makes sense. It's expensive."

"And you, do you go to school?" I ask, turning the focus back to him as we park.

He shakes his head as he turns off the ignition. "School's not for me," he says, stepping out of the truck.

I hop out of his nice truck and see the crowd of fans walking hastily to get to their seats. Azriel walks with me side by side, trying to hide the uncertainty that snakes around my chest. They can't see me in the stands, but that doesn't mean they won't know. My brother might say something, but at least I'm not here alone.

After the game, my brother meets up with us in the parking lot. The entire game left me on edge. I was terrified that the rest of the guys would notice me. Adam looked up at the stands but kept looking at Azriel curiously from the sidelines. I think he was surprised I would bring someone.

"Hey," Adam greets, his eyes flicking between us. "Wanna grab something to eat?"

I look at Azriel, but he's looking around at the crowd of people walking out of stadium getting inside their cars. Some meet up with friends; others drive off.

My brother played great, just like I knew he would, and Ohio won. I cheered despite the fear clawing in my gut, hoping Zack and the others wouldn't recognize me. I sat down the whole time and only stood up when my brother threw the ball, which was caught by one of the guys. It was hard, but I was glad Azriel was here with me.

Azriel smiled, and I noticed he would look good if his acne didn't cloud his face. He has natural blond highlights in his hair. When the light shines, it looks brighter. He has broad shoulders. He's lean and tall. Maybe a good skin routine is what he needs to clear his face a bit and boost his confidence. I think it would make a huge difference. I noticed he likes to put the hood of his sweater over his head to hide the side of his face when he's out in public.

"Yeah, sure. If it's okay with Azriel," I say, hoping he's up for it.

Adam extends his hand. "I'm sorry. I'm Adam."

Azriel shakes Adam's hand. "Nice to meet you. I work with Melody at the hardware store."

"Oh...yeah. I remember seeing you at the hardware store with Melody.' My brother glances at me in surprise and says that it's the same guy he saw when he visited the first time. "I thought you guys went to school together?"

"I'm not cut out for college," Azriel says.

"Ay, man, that's cool. Schools are not for everyone," Adam says, lightening up the mood.

Azriel smiles.

"Want to hang out with us, Azriel?" My brother asks, lightening up the mood.

"Sure," Azriel agrees.

We are seated in a corner booth at the diner. Dorothy smiles and waves at me from behind the counter.

It's a bit crowded with all the Ohio students and the fans from Colorado.

"You guys' obliterated Colorado," I tell Adam, not caring much about the win, but I want my brother to know I support him. I don't want him to worry about how I feel that Zack was on the same team, and I'm hung up about it.

"Yeah," Adam says with pride.

The door of the diner swings open, and in walks Zack and several teammates—a sight that sends a chill down my spine. My gaze darts around, trying to identify any of the faces from that night, but recognition eludes me.

Zack strides over. "What's up, man? "You were on fire out there," he booms, slapping Adam on the back.

I shrink in my seat.

Zack's gaze eventually finds me, and it's like a spotlight I can't escape. There's a look in his eyes—a knowing glint that sets my heart racing, dread coiling tightly in my stomach.

I force myself to look away, focusing on the saltshaker on the table, as Adam engages in a curt exchange about the game. My hands slide under the table, clasping each other to keep them from trembling.

"Who's your friend?" Zack asks with amusement in his tone.

My eyes lift, and I realize it is why he came over. He wants to know who Azriel is and to give him a hard time.

"I'm Azriel, but I didn't catch your name," he says with gravity, his gaze steady.

Azriel reaches for my hand, bringing it to the table and intertwining his fingers with mine. The gesture, both bold and comforting, anchors me, slowing my racing heart to a steadier rhythm.

Zack's gaze flickers to our joined hands, a flash of surprise crossing his features before he masks it with indifference. "Zack," he finally says, his eyes shifting between Azriel and me.

I want to throw salt in his eyes, hoping it will burn. I'm surprised at how well Azriel is dealing with him. I thought he would be nervous, but he's calm, supportive, and collected.

"Oh, that explains a lot," Azriel says.

Zack glances at him. A challenge in his eyes. "Explains what exactly?"

Azriel points to the large booth at the other end of the diner. Seven other football players are looking over here with smirks on their faces.

Zack glances at the table with his friends, then returns his gaze to Azriel, a smirk on his face. "You should get that fixed. Visit a dermatologist. Your face reminds me of burnt pizza."

"Fuck off," I snap. "Go sit with your girlfriends. He's not your type, Zack."

Zack laughs, but I know he's holding back because my brother is here.

"I think you should go, Zack," my brother says. "I'll catch up with you at practice."

"It's all good, Adam. I'm just messing with him, giving him a hard time." —he looks at Azriel—"I still have a soft spot for Melody, and she knows that." He gives me a wink and then turns to Adam. "Not coming to the party, dude?"

"Nah, I'll pass," Adam says in a tight voice. "I'm trying to spend time with Melody."

My brother is two seconds from telling him to fuck off. I know he is trying to be civil, but he knows that Zack has everything to do with me being kicked off campus. Zack and the rest of the team got what they wanted. Adam needs to be a team player. I can let my mistakes get in the way of his game or hinder his future.

I give Adam a grin, letting him know that I'm fine. Everything is good. I wish the lies I spilled were true. I wish I didn't have to lie to save my brother's dreams. I kept a secret that could destroy him, but I need to save him. Some secrets are better left unsaid, so the truth doesn't destroy the happiness you're trying to preserve.

"Alright, man," Zack says, "I'll catch you later."

"Yeah, you do that," Adam says in a hard tone.

"See you later, Melody." I roll my eyes.

"Hey, Az... whatever your name is. I was just messing around."

"It's Azriel." Azriel releases my hand and places his arm behind me along the edge of the booth. No problem, Zack. Have fun eating with your boys. Celebrate the win."

Zack's jaw hardens, and then he walks away.

Adam grins at Azriel. "Thanks, man."

"No problem. That guy is a dick. I'm surprised you have to play with that asshole."

"Trust me. It's not easy, but Melody doesn't want me to break his face. Trust me, I tried to convince her, but she doesn't want me to mess up my chances playing ball and lose my scholarship over it."

"That sucks, but I get it. College isn't cheap."

"Dude, neither is life. Nice truck."

"Thanks," Azriel says, and he picks up the menu.

I don't think he wants to talk about how he could afford it.

After we eat and Azriel surprises me and my brother by paying the bill, we say goodbye to my brother, promising to catch up next week.

Azriel walks me to his truck and says, before opening the door, "Your brother is cool."

"Yeah, I'm lucky to have him," I admit before getting inside.

He shuts the door, and I wait for him to get in.

My heart skips as the driver's side door remains closed, an uneasy feeling creeping over me. Turning towards the rear window, the muffled sounds of confrontation reach my ears before my eyes confirm my worst fears. Zack and four of his team-mates have cornered Azriel.

As I force the door open, my adrenaline surges and I murmur "Motherfucker."

Rounding the back of the truck, the scene before me sharpens into focus—Azriel, standing outnumbered.

"Stop it. All of you. Azriel, get in the truck," I command, my voice ringing with authority I barely recognize.

"Aww. You need a girl to save you, bitch," one of them sneers.

"Melody, get in the truck," Azriel counters in a firm command. "Now."

"It's all good, Melody. We're just having a friendly chat," Zack claims, his smile stretching wide and a hollow promise hanging in the air. "Trust me, baby."

"You sick bastard," I scorn.

Zack blinks like I slapped him.

The rumble of Azriel's truck starting cuts through the tension. The remote start's growl is a stark reminder of the odds stacked against us. It's evident from the predatory gleam in their eyes—they're not here for words. Azriel is their target because of me, and I can't let that happen.

I pull my phone out and dial. "Who is she calling?" one of them says.

"Call the cops, and I'll spin this on you, Melody," Zack threatens, confident in his ability to manipulate the narrative. "They'll take my side."

Asshole.

He's right, but I'm not calling the cops. I'm calling someone I never thought I would call.

He answers on the second ring. "Where are you?" He demands.

"On the Edge Diner. My friend is with me, and we're in trouble. I need you. Please," I plead.

Tears sting my eyes. I would never be able to forgive myself if something happened to Azriel.

He hangs up, and I stand in front of Azriel.

"What are you doing, Melody?" Zack asks.

Azriel gets closer and whispers, "I got it, Melody. Take my

keys and get back in my truck. If anything happens, you drive down the road and call the cops."

"I'm not leaving you here," I assert, looking at them defiantly.

I feel like I'm in one of those movies where the bullies surround the new kid to beat him up.

"You think this is funny?" I challenge.

"Yeah, we think it's hilarious," one of them retorts, arrogance dripping from his words. "Your little boyfriend here thought he could step on Zack and us."

"Zack came to our table, not the other way around," I counter, desperation creeping into my voice as I assess the daunting physical disparity between Azriel and them. These guys are built for the gridiron—broad shoulders with muscular builds. Despite his own physical capabilities, Azriel is outnumbered and outmatched. The reality of the situation is a heavy weight in my chest—it's five against one.

Suddenly, a familiar voice cuts through the tension: "Catch the game tonight?"

They all look up and step back.

"Shit," Zack mouths.

The other three guys give each other hurried glances that spell, Let's get the fuck out of here.

I turn to see Valen approaching, his presence like a beacon in the darkness. Clad in black, from his jeans to his sweater, he moves with purpose, his wallet chain swaying with each step.

"What's up, man?" One of the guys says recognition is flickering in his eyes.

"Nothing," Valen replies casually, but he makes a point not to look directly at me. "I came to get a bite to eat and saw you guys out here." He looks at Zack. "What the fuck is going on?"

"Let's go," Azriel says softly.

I don't think twice, walk briskly to the truck, and get inside. They know Valen, and that's one of the reasons I don't trust him, but his showing up as soon as I called means a lot right now. I think it means he wouldn't let anyone hurt me.

As we drive away, the silence between us is heavy. I don't know what to say. You were great. Thanks for coming. I'm sorry my ex-boyfriend and his *ropy* teammates wanted to kick your ass for being around me.

"I'm sorry... for everything that happened back there." I finally break the silence, my voice barely above a whisper.

"That wasn't your fault."

What bothers me is that he didn't ask about Valen or who he was. Does he know who he is? Kenyan is an old town with an even older school that is the center of it all. He grew up here and knows Mr. Crosby. I'm sure he knows who Valen is.

These people have wealth and control. It's probably why he didn't ask or hesitate to get the hell out of there. He's probably afraid of him too.

"It feels like it is," I confess, the guilt casting a constant shadow. "I should have considered the possibility of running into him... I just didn't think."

Azriel's insight cuts deeper than I expected. "He's not over you—that much is clear," he observes, reading the situation with an acuity that surprises me.

His words are a balm and a reminder of the complexities of human emotions—of Zack's twisted version of love, of my own traumas, and of the invisible scars that dictate my every interaction and my every fear.

I snort. "Love is a strong word. It's more like he wants to make me pay for getting him kicked off the team his freshman year and most of his sophomore year."

"He's older?"

"Yeah, he graduated a year before me. We dated in high school and snuck around after my parents caught him in my room one night." I pause. "He cheated on me, or I thought he did, at the initiation party with some random girl." I shake my head. "He doesn't love me, Azriel. He wants to hurt me."

"That's not what I saw. Not the way he was looking at you when you weren't looking. He's in love with you on top of whatever sick game he's involved in, but the good part is that he's out of your life because you're smart enough to keep him out."

If he only knew how injudicious I am. How impetuous and messed up my decisions are.

I can't have sex. I can't bring myself to orgasm without thinking about what they did to me. I'm messed up. Even thinking about a guy touching me, I freeze. My belly turns into knots.

Except with Valen.

After I picked up my car from the hardware store, Azriel insisted he follow me home. He pulls on the dirt road behind me, leading to the trailer.

When I get out, he rolls his window down, angles his head, and looks at the old rectangular box on the bricks.

"I think you should move from here. Mr. Crosby is old and might not get to you in time if someone were to break in. I don't think it's safe."

He means Zack and his teammates. He does have a point.

I'm safe until they find out where I'm staying. It's one of my fears. What keeps me awake at night? It doesn't help the triggers for my anxiety. The thoughts that pop up in my head. The way I felt that night when they loaded my drink and, in my absurdity, drank it without a second thought. I never expected them to do what they did.

There are times when I can't get the smell of their sweat out of my mind. How they used my body. How they broke me. How did Zack let them?

They say you never forget your first love or who you lose your virginity to. I didn't have a first love. I had my first real nightmare, and it derives inside my head, gripping me in a vice and making me want to let go. It doesn't matter how hard I try. I feel, but I can't see. Like a smoke screen was placed in front of my eyes, I heard voices coming in and out.

"Yeah, well. I don't have another option. I can't go back home. I can't find rent that cheap anywhere else."

He pushes the hood off his head. "Why don't you stay at my place? There's a spare room. It wouldn't be any trouble. I'm clean—I have someone who helps me, and I'm not a creep or anything."

I want to laugh and hug him at the same time. He's so sweet and brave. It's a nice offer, but I don't know him. Plus, I don't know where he lives.

"I can show you where I live to ease your mind."

"Thanks, Azriel. I appreciate the offer, but I can impose it on you."

He lowers his gaze in defeat. "I don't want those guys to find out where you are staying, Melody. I didn't like the way they looked at you. You're better off at my place. I don't go out much. I don't really have friends because they all moved or are in college. I don't drink or throw parties."

I unlock the door to the trailer and look back. "I'll think about it." He nods, but I don't miss the worry in his expression. "Bye, Azriel, and thanks for following me home."

"Bye, Melody."

CHAPTER THIRTEEN

MELODY

THE NEXT DAY, the air was thick with fog. The overcast was sullen. Last night, Azriel's offer weighted heavily on my mind. It was a nice offer, but I don't know him enough, and I'm not the best judge of character. I sent a text to Valen thanking him for saving me and Azriel last night but received no response. It left me with a lingering doubt.

What happened? Did he play it out? Did he say something to them about me?

I parked in the lot but didn't miss the crowd gathered in the mist of the dense fog. A guy runs to the male dorms. One of the female students is sobbing, while another is holding her hand as they walk away from the crowd. Another screams. Girls are crying with trembling hands covering their mouths. Tears run down their cheeks.

When the crowd parts, the swirl of fog goes with them. I see a dead guy sitting at the foot of a tree. His throat was cut. His eyes were staring into nothing. His mouth widened unnaturally due to the split. A pool of blood was underneath him. He is wearing an Ohio football sweatshirt. I recognize him from the Ohio football team. The words written over the white part of the sweater are in his own blood.

GOOD GAME

People begin to fire questions at me.

"Do you know him?"

"Who is he?"

"He doesn't go here. He's from Ohio. Football team, I think."

All I can think about is that he was with Zack last night. In the parking lot after we left the diner.

He's one of the guys who surrounded Azriel to beat him up.

I don't know him.

I was there, but I don't know him.

By the time I walked out of my last class, there was a swarm of police cars. State, campus, and local police surrounded the area. Some are by the tree near the dorms.

Everyone had to show their ID when asked. The discovery of a dead student in front of a tree has sparked a frenzy on social media. The irony that the tree was near the church and the cemetery gives it an eerie feel to the whole thing. No one on campus really knew who he was after reading the breaking news article. His name was Gary Clark, and he was the starting tight end for the Ohio State football team.

I called my brother, and he said he couldn't talk. He did say that the entire football team was being questioned. They went to a party last night around the time I was home. I was relieved because that would mean it happened after he was seen at the party, and who knows what those guys were into? Adam assured me that he was good and had nothing to do with it. No one liked Gary except his teammates. Adam mentioned he was a hard-ass and drank a lot. He was considered a party animal.

"Hey." I turn around and see Rose standing behind me. "Did you hear about that guy?"

"I saw."

"Damn," she says, surprised. "Sucks."

I don't want to tell her that I saw him last night at the diner. I don't want anyone to know it now, or people will talk and ask questions. Questions I don't have the answers to.

You didn't know him, Melody.

"I want to go to Babylon. I'm not hungry," she points out. "But it beats being alone in the dorm, and the cops are everywhere."

I don't want to be alone right now. I agree.

"Alright."

We walk in, and people are hanging out in tight groups. Most likely talking about the dead Ohio student. It's being aired on the big-screen TVs hanging over the bar.

"No one knows who did it. No suspects, and you can bet even if anyone in Kenyan did, they would be tight-lipped about that shit around here."

I take a seat in the farthest booth toward the back. "What makes you say that?"

"You know... bad rap for the school. They keep everything that has to do with this school under control."

I nod, and I couldn't agree more. Most Ivy League schools do. Like the people who go here. The rich kids who come here have more secrets than the government.

"What do you think?"

She scans the bar and then the door, like she's thinking about it. "I'm not sure, but it was obviously a message."

"Like what?" I asked curiously.

"Whoever did it wanted someone here to see it. That much is obvious."

"But who knew him?"

As soon as the words leave my mouth, the door to the bar swings open, and my answer walks in. They know who that guy is, but they stroll in like it's just another day at college and a dead football player from a rival school wasn't scraped off the bark of the tree across the street.

Valen, Garret, and the rest of the swim team walk in, heading toward the pool tables.

"Is that all they do?" Rose asks. "Play pool?"

"I guess there isn't much to do after school. They don't strike me as the type of guys who play video games."

Rose snorts, looking over her shoulder directly at Garret while he chats up some girl with dark hair to her waist and low-waisted jeans who does nothing to hide the string of her pants over her hips.

I glance at the TV to avoid glancing at Valen. He didn't answer my texts, and I don't want him to think I showed up here because I'm stalking him. A picture pops up of Gary. It looks like a high school picture. He looks nothing like the asshole I saw in the parking lot, but he is a good all-American high school kid who has loved playing football since he was five. It's interesting how people tend to portray someone's life story after their death. This good guy had a future. All I can remember of him was being an asshole and wanting to beat up another guy because another asshole on his team said it was a good idea. There are more highlights and a clip of his parents crying and pleading for justice for their innocent son. I was hoping they could find the killer.

A male voice interrupts my inner thoughts. "Did you see what happened?"

I look to my right. Valen and Garret stand beside the wood table. "Who hasn't?" Rose replies. "It's all over the news. Melody saw him all cut up, sitting against the tree."

"Whoa. That must have been intense," Garret says, his face pallid, sliding into the bench across from us.

"Go right ahead. Have a seat," Rose says sarcastically.

"I thought you wouldn't mind since you've been watching me since we walked in," Garret says.

Rose rolls her eyes. "You're so full of yourself. I wasn't looking at you."

"Who were you looking at then?" he challenges.

"Not you," Rose fires back. "I was looking at your friend. The one with the dark hair and piercings. I think he's hot."

She wasn't, but I don't miss the way Garret's jaw hardens or the way he glares at the guy currently playing pool with the rest of the guys.

"Are you alright?" Valen asks.

He means if I'm okay seeing Gary dead.

"Why would you care?"

"Not everyone takes seeing things like that very well."

"He's dead. I don't think you're supposed to."

"Do you want to talk about it? Alone," he asks suggestively.

Silence blankets between us for a beat. The tension grows thick.

"Go ahead. I'll catch up with you later," Rose says, breaking the awkward tension.

I slide out of the booth and follow Valen through the back exit.

"What?" I snap, leaning on the brick wall.

"Why are you mad?" Valen says this in a soft voice, placing his hand flat on the wall above me.

"I'm not mad."

"Scared?"

"I'm not."

His head dips. "You're mad at me."

I look to my left and right and notice we are alone. The sun is just beginning to set. I'm trying to hide the fact that I am upset that he didn't text me back after last night. He didn't tell me what happened, but in a way, I'm glad he didn't because one of the guys ended up dead.

"I'm..."

"You're mad because I didn't call you back. I was...busy."

A chill runs down my spine. He couldn't mean what I think...

"Doing what?"

He chuckles lightly. "I was doing homework."

"Homework?"

"I had a paper due. It's my senior year."

Fuck, right. Homework. What I'm supposed to be doing instead of worrying about why he didn't call me. Walking on campus and finding a dead body, not knowing if it's connected to me or not.

I sigh. "I know. I'm sorry. You don't owe me."

"Why didn't you ask me to go with you?"

"You mean to the game?"

He nods.

"Jealous?"

"Maybe?"

"He's just a friend from work. I didn't think football was your thing. Adam never mentioned you going to a game. I didn't think you were interested."

"I'm not. I was interested in going with you."

A flush creeps up my neck. Is he flirting with me?

"Maybe next time."

"How about I take you out?"

"When?" I find myself asking.

"Right now."

"Where?"

"I was thinking away from here. There are cops everywhere."

There are. The investigation has prompted the state police to step in, and chaos is currently raging on campus. I'm sure rumors will be running rampant by the same time tomorrow if they haven't found who did it.

"Alright."

"Alright," he repeats, lowering his head.

I look up, and before I know what is happening, his lips find mine. His hand wraps around my throat. We kiss. His tongue slides past my lips. My hands land on his hard chest. My tongue flicks the piercing on the corner of his lip. His hand wraps around my throat.

When we break the kiss, I'm stunned that it happened—that he kissed me.

"Let's go," he says softly, walking away.

My fingertips touch my swollen lips as I watch him walk toward his black Porsche. When the lights flash in greeting as he unlocks the car and opens the door, I drop my hands.

He drives away from campus. Away from the flashing lights and caution tape tied around the tree and the light post.

"It's crazy."

"What is?" he asks, looking straight ahead.

"That he died." I glance at him. "The way he died."

"Shit happens."

"It doesn't bother you?"

"I mean... It's fucked up. I didn't know him. All I know is what everyone else does. That he played football for Ohio."

"You didn't know him like you do Adam?"

He shakes his head. "Nah, not like that." He glances at me briefly. "You?"

I shake my head. "No. All I know is that he played football with Adam and hung around Zack. He was an asshole. I thought you would know more since you hung out at their frat parties."

"Is that what you think? That they are my friends."

"Aren't they?"

"No. Just because you saw me there when you weren't supposed to be there doesn't mean I'm friends with them. We don't go fishing together."

"It's no secret why I was there. I think everyone there made the fact that I wasn't supposed to be there a bigger deal than what it was."

"I'm glad you were there."

I furrow my brow. "But I thought you said..."

"If you weren't there, I wouldn't have known you existed. It wasn't like Adam would have introduced me to his much younger, underage little sister." He laughs. "I was glad Zack cheated on you, though. I know it sounds fucked up, but it's the truth."

"Why would you say that?"

"Because I'm fucked up, Melody."

"What do you mean?"

"I think you know."

"I don't."

I do, but I don't want to admit that part to him. I don't want to admit that part to myself.

"Do you like burgers?" he asks, changing the subject.

"Burgers?" He turns right into a fast food drive-through. "Yeah, who doesn't?"

He buys us both burgers. Then he drives down a secluded road, turns left, and stops in front of a lake.

"Why are we here?"

He pushes a button, and the car's rooftop retreats, revealing a sky so densely sprinkled with stars that it nearly swallows the dark. "You said you liked the stars in the summer sky. It's not summer, but it's the best I could do."

I want to melt. I want to cry. He heard every word.

Maybe that's why he wanted to read it before I turned it in to the professor. He wanted to read my thoughts.

I look up and smile. "Thank you."

"For?" He pauses between bites, his casual demeanor belying the depth of the moment.

The stars gleam with a brilliance that seems to intensify with each passing second. I pivot in my seat, facing him fully. "For listening."

"Is that what you like... for me to listen?"

"It's part of it, but I'm curious... why me?"

His response is to sip from his drink. "You'll find out soon enough."

"Is this your way of trying to get me to sleep with you?"

He's smooth; I'll give him that. He has this way of making me forget everything else. I want him, but I know it's dangerous to want someone like Valen. He's dark and unpredictable.

"Is that what you want?"

"It's obvious that's what you want." The accusation hangs between us, presenting a challenge.

The corner of his mouth lifts into a sexy grin. "Why lie? But I didn't bring you out here to fuck you."

"Why did you?"

"Because I wanted to be the one you spent your time with under the stars," he teases with a playful lilt in his voice.

My heart flips. A little laugh escapes my throat. "You want me to fall in love with you?"

His gaze lingers on my lips, intensifying the moment. The

food forgotten, my heartbeat seems to echo above the wind's whispers and the distant chirps of crickets.

As the silence stretches, my thoughts wander to the reflection of the moon on the lake, casting a silver glow that dances across the water's surface. The soft ripples, the wind's caress, the memory of a kiss that left tingles lingering on my lips. But then...

What am I doing?

A guy like Valen must have countless girls fall for him. He could never fall in love with a girl like me.

Sleep with me, maybe?

Say the right things, always.

It's what guys like him do. It's in their DNA. We both know I'm not his type, and I'm sure it's one of the reasons my brother warned me to stay away so I don't end up being one of the girls he leaves depressed with a broken heart. It would make sense for my brother to worry after the way I reacted to Zack.

"What are you thinking about?"

I inwardly cringe within myself. He purposely ignored my last question. Of course he would.

Don't fall for it, Melody?

"I'm thinking... It's getting late, and I should be heading back."

His gaze drifts to the lake, contemplative, as if weighing his next words. I should have never left with him. I shouldn't have let him kiss me.

But I did.

After he follows me to my trailer, I push down the embarrassment that he can see how I live.

"You should really think about moving," he suggests.

I snort. "You sound like my brother."

"And I'm sure everyone who visits you."

I open the small door. "Except my landlord."

He looks toward the old house, with the broken-down Plymouth still parked over the cracked driveway and overgrown grass.

"He's still alive?" he teases. "I thought old man Crosby kicked the bucket."

"You know him?" I asked, my curiosity piqued.

"Who doesn't. He's like a hundred years old, but a nice old man. He likes you if he lets you stay on his property, and he likes the fact that you're paying him. I hope he isn't hustling you."

I shake my head. "Why does everyone have a problem with where I live?"

"Why did you move out of your parents' house?"

"The same reason all kids leave their parents' house."

"Ahh, rules and freedom."

"Do you live with yours?"

"No."

"How come? Rules?"

"Something like that."

"We aren't that different."

He looks at the trailer, then back at me. "Stay with me."

I look up at the star-lit sky and laugh. "Nice try, but I think I'm safer in my banged-up old trailer."

"Are you afraid of me, Melody? I promise not to bite."

It's me I don't trust, but I don't tell him that.

"I don't know... do you, Valen?"

His smile is enigmatic, but he plays dumb when he says, "I'll bite if you want me to and to ease your mind. You shouldn't be afraid of me. It's pointless."

"Oh yeah."

He nods, confident. "I get what I want, Melody. And what I want, you'll see."

"What is it that you want, Valen?"

He nudges his chin. "Get inside. It's getting late."

CHAPTER FOURTEEN

MELODY

"WHAT MOVIES DO you like to watch?"

Azriel shrugs, placing the batteries back on the shelf, his attention only half on me. "Whatever's interesting, I guess."

"Horror? Action?"

"I like horror. If it's good."

"You?"

"I like scary. When I could watch it."

"How come?"

I glance away, the question more loaded than I intended. "I had to move out of my parents' house. The constant fighting and the suffocating rules were too much. I'm not exactly the favorite, as you can tell."

Brother can do no wrong?"

A laugh, bitter and short, escapes me. "Exactly."

"I know how you feel. Hey, want to watch a movie tonight? After work? I think Netflix added the latest *Friday The 13th*."

"Do you want me to come over to your place?"

He looks up in surprise. "You want to see it?" Azriel stammers.

I shrug. "Sure. If you promise not to be a murderer."

"Alright," he says with a smile.

He places the car in reverse and backs out of the parking lot of the hardware store. He said I could pick up my car later, and he would drive me home. I didn't want my brother stopping by and finding my car there, knowing I left with someone else in their car. It's Friday night. I'm sure he's out doing something, or maybe not. With one of the guys found murdered, I'm sure they are on lockdown anyway. Which means so are Zack and his stupid friends.

"I have plenty of room. Mrs. Mallory will stop by in the morning. She always drops in on Saturdays to clean and make me breakfast," he rambles on nervously.

I don't think Azriel has many people coming over to his house.

"Who is Mrs. Mallory?"

He scratches his brow and keeps one hand on the steering wheel. "She takes care of the house. She's kind of like a mom slash grandma. You'll really like her."

"You live alone?"

He nods. "Most of the time."

He presses the music app onto the screen. Three Days Grace's "Never Too Late" begins to play.

We drive past Kenyan and notice an uptick in campus security in an upscale neighborhood behind the university. It's secluded and dark.

He makes a right, then a left, and drives down a dark road to a large metal gate. No houses are on either side, hidden behind thick greenery, ancient trees, and sprawling branches. There are two black lampposts on each side of the large pillars. He pushes one of the three buttons on the visor. The gate swings open, and he drives through the winding path leading to a large modern home.

"Wow," I whisper in awe.

The house is gorgeous. Well-lit with white walls and black windows. Clear-encased light fixtures separate all six garage spaces.

"You live here?"

"Yep. I told you I had a lot of space."

"How..."

But I stop myself. It's none of my business. I think Mr. Crosby said his father owns the hardware store, but I have never seen him. Maybe he left the business to Azriel. It's not far-fetched. Azriel is what? Twenty-one. His parents must have had money or something. Everyone born in Kenya has money. They have history.

"Don't worry. I'm not a drug dealer or anything. I swear. You can check."

I grin. "I believe you, Azriel. I never expected this. You have a nice home."

He smiles at the compliment. "You should check out the inside. I have a pool. You can jump in if you want. It's heated." He gets out.

I don't think Azriel hangs out with people all that much. He keeps to himself, and maybe he is better off with people who love him. Veronica has had her share of assholes with the life she has lived, and she has lived here all her life. I don't know all the details about her husband or exactly what went down, and Adam doesn't tell me much.

All I know is that she had it rough before she married her husband, Alaric. I kept in touch until the night when my life turned upside down, and I changed. It's like I stood in the middle of a blackout when the light turned back on, and everything shifted focus. My perception is different.

I stopped calling. I got a new phone. I moved out of my parents' house. Everything happened so fast in the past seven months. I can't believe I'm here and not in my room planning how I'm not going to tell my parents I'm going out to a party to find a cute boy I want to fuck.

He opens the door with his phone and lets me walk in first before he closes the door behind me. I'm greeted with white-washed hardwood floors, nude-colored walls, and modern furniture. The red-lit pool is clearly visible through the floor-to-ceiling windows. The house smells like vanilla and cedarwood. It's clean and comfortable. It's probably the nicest house I've ever been in.

I like that it's hidden. It's like a celebrity lives here. Safe and sophisticated. It looks like nothing Azriel would pick out for a home.

When I glance at him, I see his innocence, but I can tell

there is also fearlessness about how he does things. The way he stood up for me against Zack and the guys. He held my hand when he knew I needed it at the table in front of my brother. He didn't hesitate. The way he talked to Zack. It showed me he cared. It showed me he was my friend, and I shouldn't be afraid.

"Azriel?" I call out.

Lost in my thoughts, I didn't see where he went. The lights turn on, eliminating the darkness in the huge kitchen with white marble countertops and white wood cabinets.

He opens the fridge. "Yeah," he says, reaching inside.

"Thank you for bringing me here. For sharing your home with me."

He hands me a bottle of water. "No problem," he says, lowering his gaze.

"Hey, are you okay?"

He gives me a small smile. "Yeah, I'm not used to having anyone over."

"Oh," I say, bewildered. "Well, I'm glad you invited me."

He gives me a tour of the impressive home but respectfully leaves out his bedroom and the main bedroom. He shows me the guest bedroom. It has a queen bed with two large nightstands and a walk-in closet. A large floor-length mirror was nailed to the wall. It has access to a bathroom with a free-standing tub and double vanity.

"You can stay in this room. No one has ever used this room. It would be a shame to have you stay in the trailer instead of here. It's perfect, and I think you'll be safer. And..."

"You won't be alone."

"I guess we both get something. You get a place, and I get someone to hang out with after work. There's internet and a study to do homework. I hope I'm not offending you with where you live, but I thought— "

"You've thought this through," I tease him, playfully lightening the mood.

He flicks off the light in the bathroom. "I didn't give it much thought because I didn't need to."

My chest squeezes.

"Thank you, Azriel. I'll think about it."

"Take all the time you need. It's here if you want it."

I feel like I'm floating. I'm warm. I feel safe, like nothing could get me. Not the nightmares. Not the memories that plague me or the need to run. The weird smell on my hands from scrubbing my skin instead causes tingles like feathers, awakening all my nerve endings.

I don't know where I am, and then it all comes back to me. The popcorn. The scary movie I couldn't say no to when Azriel suggested watching *The Conjuring* after *Friday, the 13th*, and I ended up falling asleep on the loveseat.

I peel my eyes open. My tongue stuck to the roof of my mouth because of all the popcorn, soda, and candy Azriel offered. It was like he had a snack machine. He had every candy there was.

When my eyes adjust to the stream of light coming through the curtains, I recognize the linen curtains. I'm in the guest room.

I feel something large and hard next to me. My head snaps to my right, and my heart drops. Hazel eyes look straight at me.

"You're beautiful when you sleep."

I scoot to the edge of the bed and look down. I sigh in relief that my clothes are still on. The only thing missing are my shoes.

Panic sets in my veins.

"How did you...?"

"The same way you did, the front door."

I look around. "Where's Azriel? If you hurt him, I'll—"

He chuckles. "He's sleeping in his room." He places the palm of his hand under his cheek and holds his head with his elbow bent on the bed. "He likes you, and that's a lot. He doesn't like anyone."

I'm standing on the side of the bed when I ask, "How do you know him?"

"Get back in bed, and I'll tell you."

I shake my head. "I can't."

"I've taken care of my hard work three times. All in your name. I'm good for a while."

"Very funny," I mock.

"I don't joke when it comes to getting away from the thought of you. Get back in bed, and I'll tell you."

I sit on the bed and mimic the way he is stretching out on the bed.

He pushes off and leans close. His eyes glide slowly over my face. "Azriel is my little brother. My mother died giving birth to him. My father blamed it on him and disowned him. Since he is technically the son of one of the founding fathers of Kenya, he is still entitled, but not in my father's eyes. I was too young to take care of him until I turned fifteen and took matters into my own hands. Azriel lived with the housekeeper my mother employed to take care of us before her death until I was able to step in."

My heart aches for Azriel. It's why he feels so alone.

"I asked Azriel to bring you here and look out for you at the hardware store. That's why he was ready to defend you against that prick of an ex-boyfriend of yours. Why did he agree to go wherever you asked without making it obvious? They thought they would be able to kick my little brother's ass." Valen grins, but it doesn't reach his eyes. "I taught him how to defend himself, and I made a promise to him. No one would be able to hurt him, but he needs to keep to himself and not show up in places where they will recognize him. Azriel is a Vikiar, Melody. He's the legitimate son of a Kenyan."

"I thought you were the last son of your generation."

"Not the case for Azriel. Most people don't know he exists, and I plan to keep it that way. And he doesn't need to attend Kenyan."

I have so many questions I want to ask, but I start with, "Is this your house?"

"One of them. This is my main home. Azriel lives where I do, and for now, this is it. He wants for nothing, and he likes working at the hardware store."

"Who owns the hardware store?" I ask.

The suspicion of how everything is falling into place nags in the back of my mind.

"I do, Melody. I own the hardware store where you work, and it was my idea to have Azriel offer to have you live with us. It's not safe in the trailer. I didn't want your brother to find out what I'd done. I didn't want him to know how I felt about you."

His words nag in the back of my mind. *I get what I want. You'll see.*

I can see in his eyes that he's ashamed of his addiction. Everyone knows he sleeps around.

"Did you set me up? Mr. Crosby. The job at the store? Azriel?"

His eyes fall to my lips. "Not in the way that you think, but yes. I want you, Melody. Since the first time I saw you fighting for the wrong man, I've wanted you. I told you that."

Fear and anger wash over me, but the intense way he is looking at me has me holding back. I want to yell and scream at him. He doesn't have the right to control my life. I don't understand his motive. Is it sex? There is some twisted game he is trying to play.

"What do you want? Sex? A thrill to get you off? Is this a game you want to play? A campus prank for fun?" I shake my head. "I don't get it. Look at you. Look at me."

"I'm not following. I want sex, but not on a one-night stand. I brought you to the party the other day to show you my impulses." He pauses and goes on, "I'm not playing a game. Yeah, I did some shit to get you into Kenyan and away from Ohio. There are things you don't understand, Melody. All you need to know is that I want you. I want a normal fucking relationship with a girl. I've never had one that wasn't focused on sex."

"Explain it to me."

He leans over me. Everything is bright from the sun streaming between the curtains. The blue in his eyes is bright. My heart beats faster than a freight train.

"It is true that I suffer from hypersexuality, Melody. I like sex because it gives me a high, like a drug. I wasn't lying when I said it the first time."

"So the person who's with you has to accept…"

He rests his elbows on the side of my head. "No. I'm not saying that. I don't want to cheat on the person I'm with. That's what makes it so hard. After my mother died giving birth to my brother, my father spiraled. He blamed my brother for her death. My father can't look at him without remembering that she died. In his eyes, it's like he killed her."

"That is awful."

Poor Azriel.

"Mrs. Mallory took him in until I was old enough to send her money and provide for him. I had to keep him away from everyone, or my father would get angry. He would do anything to make him suffer because, in his eyes, he's suffering because of Azriel. My father never loved me. My mother was the love of his life and still is, but he spends his time having meaningless sex with random women. It's all I have ever seen. Different women." His eyes lift. "When I had sex for the first time with a woman my father brought, I liked the feeling. I was fifteen, and it was the only thing that felt good. The only thing I didn't have to work hard to get. I don't know what love is because my father never showed me what it's supposed to be like. The closest I have to love is caring for my brother. I don't know how to love a woman in the real sense. The only relationship I know is through sex, and when I'm done…"

"You move on to the next."

He nods. "Except with you. I don't want that. I want to…"

"Want to what?" I am confused.

"I want to try. I want to be the one to take you to the dark sky and burn with the stars, Melody. I want to be that."

"So you don't want to have sex?" I'm confused.

"Right now, my body says… yes. But my heart says it's not

ready, Melody." He looks away. "If you don't like me, I understand. I'll leave you alone. You can still go to school, and I'll look after you. I'll do that because I promised your brother I would, and I don't want to hurt you. I want..."

"Does he know?"

I do like him. I think he's hot, scary, and dangerous. I wouldn't know where to begin with someone like him. I don't know how far I can go without losing what's left of myself completely.

"Your brother doesn't know how I feel about you, Melody. I'm not going to lie. I'm not a good guy. I've done things I'm not proud of, but I want you." He gestures back and forth between us. "I want to explore whatever this is."

I don't know what to say. Valen Vikiar wants to date me. A guy who every girl on and off campus wants. A guy who every girl on campus has fucked. How do I compete with that?

I look away. "I didn't think I was someone you found attractive," I stammer. "I'm nothing..."

"You're gorgeous, Melody." He closes his eyes like he's in pain. "I want to show you, but... then you wouldn't believe me. It will put things in your mind you're not sure of, and when it happens, I want you to trust me. I want you to..."

"I don't know if I could, Valen. I trusted someone with my body, and they betrayed me in the worst way. I'm no good for anyone."

"He cheated because he's an idiot. I told him to stay away from you." He smiles. "He was jealous when he saw you with Azriel."

"They wanted to beat him up."

"Azriel would have handled it."

"Azriel would have handled it," I mock.

"My brother is nice, but again, like I said, he can defend himself. What kind of brother do you think I am?"

"I don't know because I don't know you."

"Get to know me."

"I'll think about it."

"Will you take our offer to stay here instead of the trailer?"

"I don't think that's a good idea, Valen." I look around the room, taking in the comfort and space compared to the trailer. What if he heard me having a nightmare or changed his mind and kicked me out?"

"I see the wheels turning in that pretty head of yours. Azriel is here, and so is Mrs. Mallory. You'll love her. It's safer. I don't like you staying in the trailer by yourself."

"What would my brother say if he found out?"

"You're renting a room. He doesn't know about Azriel."

"Who does?"

"Alaric. Only the sons of Kenyan and the founding fathers of the school know about Azriel."

"Jess?"

I regret saying her name as soon as it slipped out. I don't know why I mentioned her. It's the second time I've done it, but they have history.

"No." The curve of his mouth turns into a side grin. My cheeks heat. He knows I'm jealous. "I don't love Jess, Melody. Yes, I slept with her, but I was confused about my feelings for her. It's one of the reasons I'm holding back because I want more with you."

"I don't trust you," I admit. More to myself than to him.

"I know, but I want you to. I'm going to do everything I can so you will."

"We'll see."

AFTER I DROP Melody off at the hardware store so she can get her car, I drive toward Reid and Jess's house. When the butler lets me into their sprawling mansion right on the outskirts of Kenyan, I find Reid seated on the sofa in the family room watching *Saw X*.

"Really, dude?" I say sarcastically, "Kids live here."

He waves me away. "I can't watch it when they're here. Gia took the little one shopping with Draven. She wants them to bond or whatever."

I sit on the loveseat. "Taking advantage?"

"Yep."

I look at the oversized television screen and then see Jess walk inside from the back patio.

"Hi," she says with a smile. "How's school?"

"It's good," I tell her. But I didn't come to talk about school, and the look she gives me tells me she knows it.

"What brings you by?"

"I wanted to talk to you guys. I haven't seen you since school started."

That part is not a lie.

"What's up?" Reid pauses the movie at the part where the guy straps himself to the chair, wearing two long plastic tubes over his eyes like a vacuum.

"I wanted to talk to you about a girl."

Jess sits next to Reid with a smile on her face. She hates that I have to marry Melissa, so this topic has all her attention.

I look at her now, and it's crazy that I don't find her attractive like I used to. I don't get hard around her or think about fucking her against the wall. Ever since Melody came into the picture, I don't think about having sex unless it's with her. I thought it was because I haven't, because she's forbidden, or because she's Prey.

"What girl? Who is she?" Jess asks with interest.

I glance at Reid. "It's Melody. Adam's little sister."

Silence.

You could hear the hum of the air conditioner as it turned on. The vent was blowing cool air on my flushed skin.

I said it. I admitted it for the first time to my closest friends. Friends that are like family, my secret. A secret I've carried since the first time I laid eyes on her.

"Valen," Reid warns.

Jess has her eyebrows raised in shock.

"I know. I-I know... she's..."

"It's not that, Valen," Reid says, concern etched in his tone. "She has been through a lot with school, and she's..."

"Prey," Jess finishes for him. "You realize that bringing her on campus in Kenyan makes her a target. It wasn't what we agreed. She has to choose, and you know how that turns out with everything else."

"What do you mean? It's not like before," I say, defensively looking between them.

I can protect Melody. I will protect her.

"If Melissa finds out, you know she will do whatever it takes to destroy her. She's delicate. She's young, Valen. And you're..."

A man with satyriasis

Jess doesn't say it, but it's there, floating above us in the room. I never thought Jess would be judgmental, given everything we've been through.

"Dude, she was kicked out of Ohio by the football team. That asshole, Zack, screwed with her future and put her brother in a bad place. He has to play, look at the asshole that fucked with his little sister's future, and play football with him. He humiliated her. Hurting her is the last thing she needs. She is not like the girls you hang around with," Reid says.

He means the kind I sleep with.

"Are you saying I'm too dirty for her? I'm too fucked up to be with a girl like Melody."

"I didn't say that," Reid says defensively.

"I like her."

"You like a lot of girls, Valen. Pick one on campus, have fun, and move on to the next. It's what has always made you happy. You used to be more outgoing. You didn't care about one girl when you could have your pick. This is your senior year. Yeah, it sucks that you have to marry Melissa, but she'll let you do it. She doesn't care who you fuck. She doesn't expect anything."

"So I can't have a meaningful relationship? You guys can, but I can't."

I can't believe this. I can't believe they think I'm incapable of loving someone.

I get up, having heard enough of this bullshit. I thought they would understand. I thought Jess would understand and encourage me to have a relationship with someone.

"Where are you going?" Jess says it with a concerned edge to her voice.

"I gotta go. I have practice. Say *hi* to the munchkin for me. She's gorgeous."

I do have practice, but it's in two hours. Reid is giving me a look that says he knows this.

Jess gives me a peck on the cheek that I don't return. I fist-bump Reid and walk out.

I'm walking to my Porsche when the front door opens, and Jess rushes toward me.

"Valen, wait..." She stops in front of me with a soft expression. "I'm sorry about what I said back there. I didn't mean it the way it sounded. I can't forget the way you were with me when I was going through my own shit. I'm sorry for the way I acted. It was insensitive." She blows out a puff of air. "Melody, huh?"

I nod. "Yeah, I like her." I look at the key fob in my hand and then at her. "I want to date her. I want…"

"What?" she asks. "What is it that you want?"

"I want to be with her, Jess. I want her to fall in love with me, and I don't know how, and I'll do anything to make that happen."

"Is that why you got her the scholarship? It was you that made sure she didn't get back into Ohio, wasn't it?"

"In a way. I didn't want her to be around that asshole. There wasn't enough to get him kicked off indefinitely, and his parents are lawyers. I didn't want people sniffing around. I didn't want to draw any more attention to Melody. She's…different."

She nods. "That makes sense, but what are you going to do about Melissa? And I know Reid isn't going to ask in front of me, but was it you?"

I snort. "You didn't think I was going to marry her, did you? And no, I didn't have anything to do with the dead kid. It wasn't me. It wasn't us. As for Melissa, I'll never marry that bitch. She's horrible and a jealous crazy bitch that doesn't know if she likes dick or pussy."

Jess smiles in agreement. "I couldn't agree more." Her smile falls, like she just thought of something bad. "Make sure she doesn't know about Melody, and if she does, make sure she stays away from her Valen."

"I know."

"Does Melody know about Melissa?"

"Not yet. It would kind of ruin my chances of asking her out on a date."

Technically, lunch at my restaurant was a date, but she didn't know that.

"I guess…yeah, it would." She tucks her hair behind her ear. "Have you two?"

"Had sex?"

She nods.

"I want to. I mean, she knows I want her, and I told her my problem, and she said… she would think about it." I rush out.

Jess grins. "She turned you down?"

"The first time, yes."

"I like her. She's making you work for it. I think she would be good for you, Valen. I saw her at the diner once. She's hot, and she doesn't know it. You'll have your hands full. If you need anything from me or from us, count us in. You know that, right?"

"I know. It's why I came to talk to you guys."

She gives me a hug, and all is right again between us. I feel better. I'm confident I can make this work.

She pulls away. "Do you know who killed that guy from Ohio?"

I look at her and give the only answer I can give her. "No."

After practice, Garret walks up to me while I'm changing in the locker room. I feel relaxed after pushing myself harder than usual. I'm worked up because I need to have sex. I want to come, but the girl I want to come inside of doesn't trust me. I can't jerk off in the locker room shower after practice around a bunch of guys. I'm frustrated. I'm so fucking weak.

"Hey, man. Are you going to the party?"

Normal Valen would smile and say hell yes to alcohol and easy pussy, but I'm not that guy anymore. I want to ask Melody Price if she will go to my house and watch movies so I can kiss her lips and then go to the shower and jerk off thinking about how they would feel around my ribbed cock.

"I can't. I have plans."

He smirks. "She still turned you down, huh?"

"No."

"Liar. I still can't believe you made me take that creative writing class again. We won't get credit for it, you know."

"Fuck you," I tease. "Like you care."

"I can't. I'm straight. Now I know why you did it, but it's not like you. I'm not going to give you shit about it. It's a nice class, and I like to hear the girls read about their fantasies so I can fuck them out of it."

I shove him playfully and pull my shirt over my head. For the first time, I hate what his comment implied. What everyone thinks of me. I'm a sex-crazed maniac. One that can't be with one girl.

I can't get over how perfectly we fit when I was leaning over her in the guest bedroom of my house. I waited for my brother to hopefully convince her to come over and see the house. I knew I couldn't do it myself, so my brother, the perfect guy he is, said he would do it if he got the chance. I almost fist-punched the air when he texted me, and he got her to come to our house. I want to keep her. I want to seduce her in every way. If she only knew what I planned to do to her body.

CHAPTER SIXTEEN

MELODY

AFTER WORK ON TUESDAY, I went to Ulta and bought the best acne treatment they had in stock. I didn't care if it was expensive. I researched the best one you could buy over the counter. I saw YouTube videos and came up with a skin routine for Azriel. It was the least I could do for him after he stood up for me Friday night. Valen put him up to it, but I ultimately invited him, so I was still on the fence about the whole thing.

Deep down, it was an excuse to see Valen. I don't have class with him on Tuesdays. On Monday, he was quiet and observant. I could feel the heat of his gaze on my back, but I didn't turn around. I tried to concentrate on what the professor was saying, but all I could think about was the scent of his skin. How close he was on the bed. The way his eyes tried to stay above my chin.

The old me would have let him fuck me. Old Melody would have arched my neck and let him kiss me. Old Melody would have lifted her hips slightly, letting him know what I wanted, but that was the old me. The new me is scared. Scared that I'll freak out and be unable to come.

There are tiny moments when I want to try. To test what I feel for him. Is it fear? Or fear that I would like it too much and want him all the time.

For now, I'll never know because something else nags the back of my mind in this school. The weird glances I get from the guys. The knowing smiles from the girls when I walk by. At first, I thought it was because I was new, but it's the same people.

I pull up to the gate to Valen's house, and it swings open.

Twilight cloaks the sky as the sun sets on the horizon. The

lights on the pillars cast a glow on the driveway. I spot Azriel's truck, but disappointment fills me when I don't see Valen's black Porsche.

My stomach clenches, thinking he's out with someone else. I wouldn't be surprised. I haven't given him an answer. Then a part of me says, it was a test and if he's off fucking someone else, that I dodged a bullet.

The front door opens and Azriel appears with a smile. "Changed your mind?" he says with a grin.

I close the door to my car with the Ulta bag in hand. "Not yet, but I got you something."

His eyebrows raise in surprise. "For me?"

I walk inside. "Yeah. I hope you won't be mad, but I thought…" I trail off.

I didn't think about his feelings when the thought popped in my head. Shit. I hope he won't hate me after this. I meant well, but he could be sensitive about his acne.

Valen said he only had Mrs. Mallory as a mother figure. She's an older woman probably in her late sixties. She might not know what options are available for sensitive skin. Skin care has come a long way nowadays, but that doesn't mean he might not get offended.

"What's in the bag?"

I sit on one of the stools in the kitchen and begin taking out the items. The five-step kit, cleanser, night cream, wash pads, and exfoliator.

He looks at all the items spread out on the marble countertop. He picks up the kit and reads. I watch as recognition plays out on his features. My stomach clenches when he doesn't say anything and stares at the box. He slowly places it on the counter and then glances at all the other items.

"I thought this would be good for you to try. I hope you're not mad at me," I say in a soft voice.

He looks up. "I could never be mad at you, Melody. Thank you," he says with a soft expression. "How does it all work?"

I inwardly sigh in relief, open the box, and read the instructions. He sits on the stool next to me, and I place the items in order. I explain what each one does, how to use it, and when. He listens intently. After a skin test to make sure he isn't allergic to anything, I start to apply the cream to his skin.

After he washes his face, he sits in front of me, and I can't help but compare him to Valen. There are similarities and differences.

"Do you have a girlfriend?" I ask.

He shakes his head slowly, trying not to move so I don't get the cream in his eyes. "No."

"Have you ever had a girl..."

"No."

I pause with the cotton pad in midair. "How come?" I ask in disbelief.

He points at his face. "I don't think girls dig the pizza face."

"I've seen worse in high school. Trust me, girls would dig you."

He shrugs. "I'm not my brother."

I smile. "No, you're not. You're you, and that is all that matters. Besides, I think you're cute."

His eyes widen as soon as the words leave my mouth. "You think I'm good looking?"

I do. He is cute and sweet. He could have any girl if he would talk to one.

"Why would you think you aren't?"

"I thought I wasn't because..."

"Of you having acne on your face?"

"Almost all the guys I've come across at school have acne. Some more than others. Girls, too. Except girls are more self-conscious about the way we look all the time. We have makeup and a slew of products to choose from to cover it all up."

"I think mine is really bad."

"It's not that bad, Azriel. Nothing a good skin care routine won't fix."

"Thank you. How much do I owe you?"

"Nothing. It's my way of thanking you for the other night. You saved my ass."

"My brother did."

I wipe the side of his face. "Before...when Zack first showed up at the table."

"I knew something was wrong when he showed up. You tensed up, and the way he was looking at you, I knew it wasn't good." He pauses like he's trying to find the right words. "Did he hurt you? Physically. Did he...?" My hand pauses in midair. He looks at me, waiting.

I grab another cleansing pad so I can apply the cream to his chin. The silence is thick between us. I don't know how to answer without lying, but at the same not tell him the truth. He would tell Valen. Valen would tell Adam, and my parents would find out. I'll be humiliated. My parents would make a big deal and not let me out of the house or, worse, send me to a center for treatment. All of these would be useless because they don't make a wrong a right. It doesn't stop them from doing it again to me or someone else. The worst part is the humiliation. The pity.

They would make me tell them things about that night I'm not sure of. Things I hardly remember myself but know they happened.

Even if they confronted them, they would say I was stalking Zack and made it up. They would say I was mad that he broke up with me or spin it in a way where it was my fault. That I'm crazy and unstable. It's all of them against me.

I rub the cream with the cotton pad gently on his chin.

Our eyes meet. His friendly. Mine full of fear.

He sees the truth dancing in the depth of my eyes but doesn't say anything. There is so much silence can say that words don't. Sometimes the truth doesn't need to be said to know that something bad happened. You can feel it. It snakes up your skin and whispers in your ear.

"Does my brother know?"

"Does he know what? I ask dumbly, but I do know. He wants to know if his brother knows that I was raped by Zack and his friends. "Valen knows them. Probably better than he should. He goes to their parties. I've seen him there." I smile weakly. "Before, when I used to go to those things. The first time I went, Valen was there."

He lowers his head and stares at the ground like he's lost in thought. "You don't...go. Anymore?"

"I don't drink or go to parties anymore," I say quietly. "I don't date either."

He nods, and I think he gets it. I think he understands why I live in a trailer. Why I'm skittish. Why I don't accept his offer even though it's a good one. Because I can't trust anyone.

I start on his forehead and concentrate on his trouble spots before I have to clean up and then begin the next step.

The sound of a metal chain has me looking up. Valen leans on the wall, playing with his wallet chain with his fingers. His eyes shift between me and his brother. His jaw set. His blond hair flat and tousled. His shirt rides up, revealing the band of his Alexander McQueen boxers under his black ripped jeans and black combat boots. Valen is goth personified with his style while outside of work. Azriel is hot emo boy.

Similar but different.

"Hey, I didn't hear you come in," I say with a nervous smile.

His expression is blank. I hope I didn't overstep by stopping by without letting him know.

Azriel doesn't glance in his direction or greet him. I find it odd but don't point it out. I have no idea how they interact with each other when I'm not around.

CHAPTER SEVENTEEN

VALEN

WHEN I SAW her car in the driveway, my heart was pounding in my chest. Did she change her mind? Is she staying? When I entered quietly and saw her with my younger brother, my heart sank. The way she was taking care of him. It didn't bother her that he has acne and is full of pimples. I was also surprised he let her touch his face. He doesn't let anyone talk to him about it. I've tried, but he always changes the subject or goes to his room to play video games. I felt bad. I wanted to take him to a doctor, but he always brushed it aside and said he was fine when I knew he wasn't.

I tried not to let my jealousy get me into a chokehold. It's a foreign emotion. One that I'm not used to. One that I have to get ahold of. He's my brother, but she's the girl I want.

The one with the hair I itch to touch. The skin I wish to lick and the pussy I want to fuck. And she is currently taking care of my brother while he looks at her like she's the girl of his dreams.

There is a knot in my throat when she slides off the stool to wash her hands.

My brother won't look at me, and I know something is wrong.

He's mad.

He does this when I've upset him, and that is the last thing I want.

"Hey, man. You invited her?"

I'm fishing for information. I could easily ask her, but I want an excuse to talk to him. To feel him out. Look where his head is.

"No, she stopped by to surprise me. She went and bought me

this"—he picks up a bottle of acne cream—"for my face and came to show me how to use it."

The way he said it, I have a ball stuck in my throat.

I try to swallow and manage to say, "Oh, I had no idea she was stopping by."

"Is there a problem?" he asks with an eyebrow raised.

My lips twitch because of the funny way he looks with the white cream all over his face.

"It looks like someone jizzed on your face, but no, I don't have a problem."

"She did this for me."

"I did what?" Melody asks, walking back into the kitchen.

"Nothing," we both say in tandem.

I point to the sliding glass door and say, "I'll be outside while you two finish up."

"You don't have to go. I'm almost done," she says.

But she doesn't understand that I'm jealous. I'm jealous of her alone with my brother. I want to take her to my room, rip her clothes off, and claim her as mine. I don't want her taking care of his face or stopping by because of him. I want her to stop by because she can't stand not being around me. It's shitty of me to think this way, but there is something else that bothers me. She told him she didn't date. I caught that part when I walked in, but then there was silence. There was more I didn't catch. I want to know more. What did she say before I showed up? What did she tell him? What did he ask?

Did he ask her out, and she turned him down? Does Azriel want Melody for himself?

I jump in the pool after taking my clothes off and swim in just my boxers. I take my frustration out in the pool. Both angry and sexual. I thought of going to the shower to jerk off and think about her, but that would be weird. She's in the house with my brother, and I'm fucking myself in the next room at the thought of her.

I break the surface when I reach the end of the pool and see her watching me from the edge.

"Want to go for a swim?" I ask.

"I don't have a bathing suit."

I look down at my boxers, the imprint of my dick piercings visible underneath the water with bright red lights. "I don't either." She blushes and looks away. I take the opportunity to get closer to the edge so she can't see how hard my cock is. "Jump in. It's warm." Her eyes land on me. "There is nothing to worry about. I won't let you drown. I'm a good swimmer."

"I heard you're the best swimmer in Kenyan, possibly in the state of Ohio."

She isn't wrong. After the guys graduated, I was the best.

"You should come and see me sometime. Judge for yourself."

"You want me to see you swim?"

"Yeah, why not? Have you ever been to a swim meet?"

"I never knew a guy who swam competitively before."

"Now you do." I smile. "Will you come see me on Friday? Cheer for me?"

"You want me to cheer for you?" She laughs. "I think you have plenty of people to cheer for you."

"But I want you there, and..." I smile. "For you to tell me if I suck. If I don't, and win, you promise to let me take you out on a date."

Her smile fades, and I get nervous inside. I want her to see me swim. I want everyone to know she is there because of me. I also want to take her out on a real date with flowers and shit.

"I don't know, Valen," she stammers. I see something in her eyes. Fear. I would never hurt her. "I don't mind going to see you compete, but I'm not..."

"Are you afraid I will hurt you, Melody?"

Her eyes lift, and my stomach sinks. Dread slides in my veins. Air leaves my lungs. I've seen that look before. Not on her, but...

Her eyes are glassy. "I-I..."

No, no, no.

Who?

Then it dawns.

She is leaving her parents' house. *I don't drink. I don't go to parties. I don't date.* What she told Azriel when I walked in. At the restaurant, she was hesitant. She used to have this spark. It's what drew me in. Her fire. It's what I've been trying to find when I look at her, and I can't find it.

Rage burns in the back of my eyes. I tear my gaze from hers so she doesn't see what I feel. What I want to do.

"Who hurt you, Melody?" I ask in a pained voice.

She looks at the water, then at me. "I don't remember," she mutters.

She doesn't want to tell me or...

"Where?" I am confused.

She steps back and shakes her head slowly. "It doesn't matter," she says, giving me a tight smile. She's hiding from something or from someone. She doesn't trust anyone, but that's going to change.

"Come here," I demand.

She takes two small steps forward. I pull myself out of the water, not caring that she can see the imprint of my cock under my wet boxers plastered to my thighs. Her eyes roam appreciatively over my chest, down to my stomach, and lower.

Water drips on my skin, and my skin pebbles from the cool breeze. I reach with my hand slowly, not caring if I'm wetting her black top when I caress her bottom lip with the pad of my thumb.

"I would never hurt you, Melody. Whatever happened, I want you to know you could tell me. When you're ready, I promise, I'll make it right. You don't have to be afraid of me or Azriel. We wouldn't let anything happen to you." She steps closer. The heat from her skin caresses mine. Her lips are inches from the middle of my chest.

Her eyes dip to my erection. "I'm not going to excuse the fact that I want you," I say with a smile. "But I would never force you. I want that to sink in," I say, leaning close to her ear, "and when I find out who hurt you, nothing will stop me from taking what they loved the most. It will hurt, Melody. I promise they will remember."

She turns her head, and our lips meet. I cup her delicate face in my hands and slide my tongue between her lips, sealing my promise with my tongue. Her dainty fingers land flat on my chest. A whimper escapes her throat. I deepen the kiss, pressing my hard cock into her lower belly.

Kissing her makes me feel like time has stopped and reset. It can last forever, like a short circuit that keeps tripping over and over until I break the kiss, leaving her breathless.

Our chests are rising and falling. My heart hammers inside my chest. My cock begs for me to take her, but I won't. Not until she is ready. Until she accepts that I want her and she wants me, even if what I really want is to take her clothes off and get back in the pool so I can lay her on the lounge chair on the sun deck and lick her skin, watch her nipples harden as I suck one, then the other, while she gazes at the dark sky, recalling the moment when I caressed her skin with my tongue, just before I fucked myself and rubbed my cum over her tits like body oil.

I'm thinking this while she stares at me. Her eyes were full of lust, not wanting to let go. I was afraid of what I might do. I am afraid of what it would mean if she did it, but I need her. I need to feel her just a little.

She is the heroin, and I'm the addict, and I would do anything for a taste.

"Can I convince you to go in the pool with me?" I ask hopefully.

She must have seen the want in my gaze and the way my cock wouldn't calm down. She looks over her shoulder, probably worried that my brother will see her.

She looks back and bites her lip. "Umm..."

"You're wearing panties, aren't you?" I whisper.

She smiles and nods. It didn't matter if she wore them or not; I would still get a glimpse of her pussy and the shape of her tits.

What I've seen so far is nice. Firm upthrust breasts I want to suck on. A plump ass inside her jeans.

"It's like a bathing suit." I look down at my thin boxers molded to my thighs and my hard dick. "Only thinner, but essentially the same concept."

She agrees because she removes her shirt. I stand hypnotized, not getting back in the pool in case she changes her mind.

She pulls her jeans down her thighs and takes off her shoes and socks. Her panties stay on, like her bra. They're hot pink. It reminds me of what her pussy must look like spread open along with the cheeks of her ass when I tongue it.

I look at the sky and smile when I see the clouds move and the stars appear. I still want to be the guy she first talked about in class. The one who burns with her like the stars, but the guy who kills anyone who hurts her.

I tell myself that, in time, I'll find out. I'll start at the source. The one who called her ugly and body shamed her after she gave herself to him. The same one that looked at her like she still belonged to him. Zack.

She walks over to the shallow part of the built-in sun deck. She dips her foot to test out the water. The jets cause the water to bubble, like boiling water on a stove. It's warm, so I know she won't back out, telling me it's too cold.

I slide into the pool without making a splash when she steps in, and I feel giddy like a high school idiot about to get his first taste of pussy. She turns sideways, and my dick twitches when I notice she's wearing a thong.

She's gorgeous. Her stomach is flat and smooth, her hips flared slightly, and she has a perfect ass, with the tips of her hair hitting right above her nipples, plush lips, a straight nose, and dark lashes.

My eyes dip to the triangle part of her panties, tracing the outline of her pussy lips.

Melody is gorgeous.

"You're gorgeous," I admit. "Any man who tells you differently is a liar and doesn't want you to be with anyone else. It's what an insecure asshole says to a girl he can't keep. I think you're stunning."

"Is this your way of convincing me to sleep with you?" she teases with a grin.

"Maybe," I tease right back.

She sits in the lounge chair, touching the water bubbling on the surface with her fingers. I reach for her. My hands touch her smooth legs up her thigh.

"Is this okay?" I ask.

"Yes."

Her nipples are stiff under the thin fabric of her pink bra, sticking to her skin. Her breasts are big and firm. Perfect. She has a deep valley that I want to slide my tongue through.

My hands are on her hips. I'm on my knees, leaning slightly over her. My eyes trail her smooth skin. The strap of her bra hangs slightly off her right shoulder. I reach out and put it back in place when she surprises me by arching her back, and it falls right back. The cup of her bra barely contains her nipples.

My mouth is full of saliva. I'm fucking drooling over her. She looks hot seated on the lounger in the pool in only her pink underwear.

The tip of my tongue glides over her thighs. I savor the smell of her skin and memorize the way she tastes. A hint of strawberry and her. *My Melody*.

My tongue continues over her stomach until I reach her barely covered nipple. My eyes lift. I see the acquiescence in her gaze. I tease her soft skin with the inner part of her bottom lip. I lick. Her breath hitches, and I lick harder.

She tilts her head back and closes her eyes. I tug at her bra, freeing her heavy-set breasts. Fuck.

I suck on her tits until they are wet from my saliva and the pool water. I grip both in my hands and squeeze, sucking them like two juicy fruits. She whimpers and lifts her hips. I hold her steady and kiss her. I lick her lips, chin, neck, and then the little spot in the center of her throat.

"Play with your pussy, baby," I rasp on her skin. "Show me. Spread your cunt open for me."

She pulls her panties to the side and strums her clit. I watch, riveted, while her delicate fingers spread her pussy.

Her pussy is shaved. Lips are wet and pink. She's showing me her pink flesh. I'm dying to fuck her, but not yet.

"Mmm... Valen," she moans, her fingers working faster over her clit.

I lift my hips, pull my boxers down, and free my cock. Her brows rise in surprise. Her fingers pause, and she stares.

From the look on her face, she's never seen a pierced cock before.

I have six frenum piercings, also known as Jacob's ladder, from the base to the tip of my cock. I also have a prince albert and four rings along my scrotum, all evenly spaced, called a lorum piercing. I stroke my cock slowly. The moon caused the metal to gleam.

Her eyes lift. "Does it hurt?"

I smile. "There's only one way to find out." She licks her lower lip. "I've had no complaints," I admit.

"Did it hurt when you did it?" she asks curiously.

"The reward is worth the pain," I say, with my cock in my hand growing bigger the longer she stares at it. "You can touch it, Melody. I know you want to."

Her hand touches the first barbell, and I think I'm going to die. A drop of cum leaks from the tip. I'm so fucking horny. I want her so bad; it's taking everything in me not to take what I want.

"It's...gorgeous," she says.

I smile. "You think I have a pretty dick?"

She nods. "I think you're pretty everywhere."

"I would have preferred hot, but I'll take it."

She laughs, and I get a glimpse of her straight, milky-white teeth. She's suddenly shy, and it's refreshing. She pulls her hand away nervously.

"Can I kiss you?"

"Okay."

She looks up, and I lean in, taking her lips. "I meant whenever I want."

We kiss and kiss. I lean closer, hovering over her, my dick hard on the side of her stomach. I massage her nipples.

She whimpers, and I suck her lips, continuing to fuck her mouth with my tongue. I grind my hips, my cock rubs on her stomach, and she can feel the underside of my piercings, and it feels so fucking good.

"You feel so good, Melody. You're in control, baby. Tell me what you want."

She wraps her hand around my cock, jerking me off, surprised that she's taking control. I want to follow her pace. So I listen.

"I want to come," she says, "but..."

I'm reading her. She wants to come, but like this. No penetration.

Baby steps. I can do that.

I pull the soft fabric of her panties down her hips to her knees and spread her pussy with my fingers. My lips are a breath away.

"Is this okay? I ask.

"Yes," she says on a desperate plea.

My girl wants to come.

I eat her pussy. I take her slowly, licking her with my tongue, and hold her lips apart. She's tight as I continue with long strokes down to her asshole. She writhes and lets her legs fall to the side like she's straddling the lounger. She slides up so I can get in deeper. Her tits are wet and glistening under the moonlight. My tongue is hard. I drive it into her pussy and fuck her deep. Her hips lift, and she's now fucking my face. I play with her tits while I take her pussy deeper in my mouth. Her back is arched, and she looks beautiful. My face is full of her arousal. My chin, cheeks, and nose. She plays with her clit, my tongue sliding over her finger as I jerk my cock. Her breasts are rising and falling.

She trembles when she comes. Long and hard, causing her legs to shake. I don't stop until I suck her cum into my mouth. It's sweet.

I don't stop jerking myself off. I'm about to come and watch her spread out for me after I sucked her pussy like a mango, all swollen and ripe.

I'm on my knees, and I push my hips in when my balls tingle, signaling that I'm going to come hard.

"Melody?" I call out in a strained voice. "I'm coming."

She pushes up on her elbows. Her eyes are fixated on my cock, her mouth parts, and the first string of cum shoots out, hitting her mouth.

Fuck, that's hot.

I grunt, jerking my cock. More cum shoots out, painting her breasts. More lands on her neck.

With the head of my dick, I smear cum over her skin like the cream she was spreading over my brother's face.

When I'm done, I smile, looking at her perfect body painted with my cum.

Satisfied, I lean close and whisper, "You're mine now."

CHAPTER EIGHTEEN

MELODY

I WAKE up the next day for school, looking at the stream of light coming through the small window. For a second, I forget where I am, but then I look at the small space.

I tentatively sit up and wince from the sharp pain in my lower back. I look at the sticky notes stuck on the plastic lining of the trailer. Reminders of the assignments I need to complete. How behind I am. Shopping, helping Azriel, and then...

Memories from last night cause my stomach to flip. The pool. His magnificent cock.

I brace for the guilt I thought I would feel, but it doesn't come. Touching his thick, hard cock and the...

I blush, remembering how it felt on my fingers. How he rubbed the head over my breasts, painting his cum over my nipples like lip gloss. I admit I was scared. I was afraid he would see how fucked up I was by my reaction. But Valen proved the little voice in my head wrong. He proved to my body that it could feel.

Now I crave his touch, and it terrifies me. *He* terrifies me because he hasn't been inside me, and if I let him, I know he has the power to destroy me.

I walk into my first class of the day, and when people stare at me, it's like they know about last night. I know it's all in my head, but it doesn't quell the feeling that they know what I did with the king on campus last night. It wasn't much, but to me, it was turning the page into a new chapter.

The professor drones on about math and how you should practice it every day to avoid forgetting the steps, blah, blah, blah.

All I could remember were the steps of what Valen did last night. I've been in a trance since he followed me home after I refused to stay the night. I can't bring myself to take their offer because that would mean he would be close.

Close enough to kiss and touch me when all I can think about is how it would feel if he wanted to fuck me. I want to feel his face against my legs. How thick his lips are against mine. How thick his wicked cock would feel when he stuffed it in my pussy and made me scream.

When he pulled it out, all I could think about were the barbells disappearing inside me one by one. Would it feel good, or would it hurt a little? Or would it hurt the first time, but not the second?

The next class slides into the next until it's lunchtime, and I feel like a zombie walking toward the quad on campus. My heart is in my throat, wanting to see if he's there or not. I'm not sure if I'm ready to see him so soon or if I should lay low so I don't look desperate. I'm not sure if I could handle more.

It was the first time I could touch my body and not feel scared or hopeless because I couldn't come. Last night was the first time I could do it, and it was because of Valen. He knew where to lick, suck, stroke, and kiss me.

I didn't notice I had already reached the table until I heard the familiar voices of his friends. If I'm like this after simple foreplay, I could only imagine the state I would be in if he fucked me. Is this how women feel after he fucks them? A sex hangover?

"Hey," a guy says, waving his hand over my face like he can't tell if I'm blind or not.

I look up, and it's his friend Garret.

"What?" I ask, confused.

"You can have a seat," he says with a smile. "I've been trying to talk to you, but you kept staring at me like I wasn't here. Is everything alright?"

I nod, looking around the table. I spot Charlie flirting with a girl. She must be a senior. They all must be seniors. My eyes scan the rest of the table, but it's just Charles, Garret, and the girl.

"Yeah. Everything is fine."

But I really want to tell him nothing is fine because his friend isn't here.

He's looking at me with curious interest, and I want to blurt. *I want to fuck your friend and can't stop thinking about his amazing dick, but I'm scared of what it might mean.*

"How was class?" he asks like he's interested.

"Fine."

He stares at me for a second longer than necessary. He nods like he's thinking of what to say next, trying to find the right words.

"He should be getting here in the next five minutes. His class is about to end in the next..." He picks up his phone and says, "Three minutes."

I try to play it off by giving him an "I don't know who you're talking about" expression, but it fails. It's as if he can see right through me, but it doesn't hurt to try.

"Oh, I wasn't."

He cocks his head. "Did you come here to see me?"

"I came to eat lunch," I correct.

He looks at the table and then at me. "Where's your food?"

"I haven't bought any yet."

"When are you planning to?"

"I can't sit here?" I say carefully.

"I never said that, but you're sitting in front of me, staring at nothing with no lunch, waiting for him to show up." He leans slightly over the table and lowers his voice. "It's obvious you like him."

"I don't..."

"You have nothing to worry about. He's into you," he says proudly.

"Did he say that?"

"I'm not at liberty to discuss." He winks. "All I'm going to say is that he's into you."

"How's that?"

"What did he tell you?"

He leans forward again. "Ask him yourself."

The wind picks up like nature senses his dark presence. I follow Garret's line of sight and see Valen walking from building two this way. The conversation stops when he approaches. They begin again when he passes.

He's wearing ripped black jeans and a charcoal gray hoodie, a contrast to the ink on his neck. One sleeve rolled up, revealing a tattooed forearm lightly veined. When he reaches the side of the bench where I'm sitting, he straddles it, facing me. My cheeks blush shamelessly, trying not to look between his legs. I could smell the scent on his skin. Citrus and cedar. He looks like a famous rock star. Dark and sexy.

"How was class?" he asks, ignoring everyone else seated at the table.

"Humdrum."

"Algebra, right?"

He knows my schedule. I wonder what else he knows.

"Yes."

"You find it monotonous because it's easy."

"Are you sure it's not because I find it hard?"

"You're perspicacious. I find that hard to believe."

If he only knew, I wouldn't. If I was, I wouldn't be here.

"I'm not."

"The fact that you know what that word means..." He raises his eyebrows. "What?" His eyes shift to Valen. "I've never heard you talk to a girl like that. You always tone down the fact that you're smart. Genius even."

"I'm not," Valen says. "I'm no different from any other student here."

Garret snorts. "Yeah, tell that to your GPA or, better yet, IQ test."

"Those are biased."

"You took it anonymously. I should know; my score was average compared to yours. It was not biased. Stop hiding the fact that you're fucking smart. You're here because you're bored. The same way she feels in algebra class."

"Is that true?" I ask.

"Now that you're here, I'm not bored." The breeze pushes a strand of hair into my face. "I'm"—he slides the rogue piece of hair behind my ear—"enraptured."

Chills glide over my skin like a tidal wave from his words. My eyes are lost in the shades of his eyes to see if I'm the cause.

"There you are," a female's voice says, interrupting the moment and taking a seat next to Valen.

Valen swings his leg over and faces Garret. The air around us shifts, leaving me confused.

"What's up, Melissa?" Garret says in a flat voice.

She leans forward. Her bottled platinum blond hair frames her face. The shape of her eyes, perfect brows, high cheekbones, and shimmery lips from her pink lip gloss. Melissa is beautiful.

I can tell Valen thinks so too, because he has suddenly avoided my gaze.

"I saw Valen sitting over here and thought I should come over so we could have lunch like old times. Right, baby? Like old times," she says demurely.

Garret's gaze swings to me, to Melissa, and then to Valen. My heart sinks, but my inquisitiveness doesn't allow me to assume. I want to know the truth behind Valen's words. What did last night mean?

I smile. "Hi, I'm..."

"Melody."

She knows my name.

"Yes."

Her smile widens, but it's forced. "Everyone knows who you are."

"Yeah." I glance at Valen. "Are you ready to get something to eat?" I ask purposely, ignoring her.

His jaw hardens, but he doesn't look at me.

"Sorry, but I can't." He gets up and looks down at Melissa. "Ready?"

Melissa gets up, and I try to swallow the needles in my throat, but it stings, and it feels like all my saliva has drained from my mouth to prepare for the tears that I'm holding back.

"Yes, baby," she says with a triumphant smile. She slides her arm through Valen's as he walks away and looks over her shoulder. "It was nice meeting you, Melody. We should all hang out sometime. Show you around."

I wait until they walk toward the parking lot and watch as he opens the door to his car so she can get in. Not once did he look back. Not once did he look up when he shut the door for her.

"It's not what you think," Garret says.

I grab my bag and stand. "It's okay, Garret," I say deliberately. "I don't have to think about anything."

"You're mad because you're jealous, and he turned you down to leave with her."

"Down?" I say to play it off. His words sting with the truth, but it's better this way. It's better I know now before falling into a trap.

"I thought you weren't waiting for him."

I shake my head. "You know what? Rose was right about you. You are an asshole."

I walk away, done with people playing games with me.

He is a sex addict, Melody. You know exactly why he left.

CHAPTER NINETEEN

MELODY

TUESDAY

Wednesday

Thursday

Friday

"Are you going to answer? It's been going off again."

I grab my phone from under the counter by the register, open the messaging app, and block his number.

I place the phone back and look up. "Done."

"You want to talk about it?"

"No, Azriel. I don't," I say dryly.

I hate being standoffish with Azriel. It isn't his fault that his brother is an asshole. Valen was right about one thing: I am astute and keen. I knew the type of guy he was when I first laid eyes on him.

He didn't hide it, but, like always, I didn't listen to my instincts. I didn't listen to my brother.

Rose laid it all out that day at the bar about him. She didn't know me, and she had no reason to lie about the things she said about him. About Melissa. But I thought I was different. He knew what strings to play to get me to fall for the things he said. It didn't take much for me to take my clothes off like a desperate idiot in his pool. I could never hold a guy's attention.

I'm not *that* girl. It's why I'm fucked up. I can't remember.

"Melody?"

"Yes, Azriel."

"Are you okay?" he asks in a soft voice.

"I'm fine," I quip.

"Are you sure you want to come back, Melody?" Dorothy asks. "I mean, I love that you want to work for me, and you know I need the help, but..."

"Please, I can't work there. It's..." I trail off.

Dorothy isn't stupid. She knows I'm trying to come back because of Valen. I can't see the tortured look in Azriel's face anymore, and I hate treating him the way I have. He doesn't deserve it, but I can't be around him. He's going to expect me to talk about what is bothering me at some point, and I can't.

"Alright," she relents. "Come back. You are currently my best server, and good help is hard to find. But I'm warning you, Melody," she says in a serious tone, "he will show up. Running from him will make him chase you harder."

She means Valen.

"Who said I was running?" I lie.

"Avoiding him. Hiding. Whatever you want to call it, he will come, and he's not going to stop until he gets what he wants."

I scoff. "I'm the last thing he wants."

"You have your uniform?" she asks, and I'm grateful for the change of subject.

"Yeah."

"Good. I'm short-staffed. Can you pick up a shift?"

I smile. "Sure."

VALEN

"WHAT'S WRONG?" I ask when I walk into the kitchen.

My brother sits at the dining table, staring mindlessly at the wall. I've had a shit week trying to get Melody to talk to me without pushing her away. It's the fourth day in a row that she isn't home. I could have shown up at the hardware store to speak to her, but then my brother would know what happened. I figured everything was okay if I explained that Melissa didn't mean anything, and I would take her to lunch, dinner, or both. Except that she won't answer my calls. She skipped class, which tells me she's pissed off at me.

"Nothing," he says in a flat tone.

I take a seat and notice he hasn't touched the bowl of soup on the table—it remains untouched and cold.

I pinch the bridge of my nose. "Azriel, if there is something I should know, it's not going to do any good if you keep it from me. Is it Dad?"

"I don't have a father," he snaps. "My mother is dead, and I just realized the brother I looked up to all my life is no different from the father who can't stand the sight of me."

"What the fuck is that supposed to mean?"

He gives me a pained look. "Why?"

"Why what?" I snap.

"Why her?" he growls.

I recoil. It's the first time he's been this angry with me about a girl. This is about Melody. Is he jealous? Does he know how I feel about her? Does he want her for himself?

"I don't know what you—"

"She quit," he interrupts.

I blink. "How? Did she tell you?"

"Don't worry. She didn't tell me how you hurt her, but she doesn't have to. Her silence says what you are too cowardly to say. Whatever the fuck you did, I can only imagine how you did it."

I clench my teeth. "Go ahead"—I slam my fist on the white Italian table, causing the soup to slosh out of the bowl—"say it," I taunt.

"You used her. You treated her like you treat every fucking girl in your life. You fucked her and then acted like she meant nothing."

"I didn't..."

"It's obvious that you did, just like the bastard who fathered me." His eyes are hard, and his jaw is clenched. "You hurt her. In her eyes, you're no different from the ones who raped her."

"What did you say?" I roar, swiping the bowl of soup off the table. The bowl crashes to the floor, my chair flipping backward behind me.

My blood is boiling, causing my anger to erupt like a volcano as I lean over the table with my face inches from his.

He grins sarcastically. "I'm surprised you didn't know. You're friends with her ex and his friends. The same ones live the college life while a beautiful, innocent girl suffers because she's not from a prestigious family and didn't know any better than to trust a guy who took advantage of her. Tell me, was it worth it?"

He stands up, and I can see the disappointment, anger, and rage swirling in his eyes, mirroring my own reaction to what he said. *Rape?*

"You said she was raped? Did she tell you who it was? Was it that piece of shit boyfriend?"

"She didn't say exactly. She said she didn't remember."

"When?"

"She didn't say, but I saw it in her eyes. She doesn't drink. She doesn't go to parties, and she doesn't date. It's fucking obvious, Valen."

"Did you ask her?"

"What do you mean?" he says, confused.

"Did you ask her out?"

"Out of all the things I said, that is what you asked me. Because you're jealous?"

"Do you like her?"

"Yes," he says.

I take a deep breath. "Do you want to fuck her?"

"That is easy to answer. You beat me to it."

I'm on the fence about telling him how far I went with her, but all I can think about is how I'm going to dissect the person who touched her. *There was laughter, not that he laughed.* She didn't have to use the word *they* in class. If it's more than one, the things I would do.

We lock eyes. He's challenging me while I plot. But most importantly, I need to find her.

"Where is she?"

He sits. "I don't know, and if I did, I wouldn't tell you. She obviously doesn't want anything to do with you. What did you do?"

I look at my boots. "Melissa. She tested me, and Melody was there."

"Tested you?" he asks incredulously.

I look up. "She wanted to know if I'm interested in her or if I'm fucking her."

"You are."

"I'm not... It didn't get that far. It's not because I don't want to. I'm..."

"I was waiting for her to choose, and now she isn't interested. You realize you're bringing her here because you can't handle your overstimulating sexual fantasies, which puts her in danger."

"I'm protecting her."

He scoffs. "Yeah, from who? You? Them? The way I see it, she is bait for the wolves, and she doesn't know it. You couldn't help yourself."

"I didn't know that happened to her, but I'm going to find out."

He laughs sarcastically. "Oh, yeah. You're going to walk up to her and ask. She's going to trust you because you have shown her that your prince is charming and has a key chain for a dick. You know what? Part of me loves that she will turn you down, but then there is a part of me that knows she is in danger if she doesn't choose wisely. She's going to be in Kenyan for the next three years. I'm trying to figure out how she is going to survive because you can't see past the tip of your dick."

He's right. I fucked up. I didn't think because all I could see was her. She is all I could think about. She was young at the time, and I didn't pursue her because I'm not a sick fuck. I waited until she was older. It's a secret I kept because I couldn't balance love, sex, and a relationship. All I could do was wait.

"I know," I say, defeated. "I messed up and don't know how to fix it."

"What happened with Melissa?"

I told him.

"Where did you go?"

"I dropped her off at the stop sign and told her to get the fuck out of my car. Do you think for a second that I would choose Melissa over Melody? I chose Melissa to protect Melody from Melissa. She would destroy her, and you know it."

"She played you." He shakes his head. "She knew you would protect her. Melissa played you so that Melody would be vulnerable."

"You don't think I know that?"

"Does Melody know about Melissa? About…"

"No. She doesn't know, and what her brother does know is that he is sworn to secrecy and cannot tell her. She won't know until she chooses. She's Prey, Azriel. There are rules, and even I can't break them."

He leans his elbows on the table with his face in his hands. He can't help her, and he hates it.

"What do you plan to do?" he mumbles.

"She's Prey... and I'm the biggest predator."

"How about the other problem?" he asks, looking up curiously.

"That is where you'll help me."

He smiles, but it's like he knows something I don't.

"She's here for another reason, isn't she?"

Sometimes I wonder who's smarter.

"What do you mean?"

"She's different." He shakes his head and looks out at the pool through the glass window. "She's here because she needs to be. She's unstable right now. You know that, right?"

"It's why I'm going to need your help."

"Fine, but don't hold me back this time."

"Deal."

CHAPTER TWENTY

MELODY

"HEY, I didn't know you worked here," Rose greets me with a smile.

"You found me," I reply, mustering a grin.

She scans the crowded diner. "This is a productive way to spend your Saturday nights."

I need to make all the money I can until Zack and his idiot friends find out I'm back working here.

"What can I get you?" I ask.

"Um..." She scans the menu. "Sprite... and a salad, no dressing."

"I got it," I say, writing it down.

She looks thinner, but I don't point it out.

"Hey, want to hang out?" she asks, hopefully. "Not at a party or anything. I was thinking in my dorm. What time do you get off?"

I don't want to go back home tonight. I keep waking up in the middle of the night, not remembering where I am.

"Sure. I get off in about an hour."

AFTER MY SHIFT, I follow Rose in my car. I've never been to the female dorms on campus. It's not like I was given the grand tour like you get at most colleges. It's dark and looks like werewolves and vampires live here rather than college students. The stone facade, weathered and worn like it's been here for centuries, exudes an aura of solemnity and secrecy.

"Welcome to Drury Hall," Rose says it like a tour guide, guiding me through the hallway.

Ornate tapestries line the walls, and vintage light bulbs that glow yellow replace the once-candle sconces, spreading over the walls and casting shadows as we pass.

When we reach the second floor, I follow her into her room. Her laptop glows in the dim light, posters of pop culture icons adorn the walls, and the faint aroma of instant Ramen noodles lingers in the air.

"It's not the best," she says in a tone hinting at sarcasm.

"You should see where I live," I say, looking at the '90s vintage Bush poster. "You like Bush?"

"Are you kidding me? He's hot, and his songs are a vibe."

"I agree. I think he was one of the biggest underrated song-writers in the nineties. I love grunge rock."

She places her phone on the charger and opens the music app to "Glycerin" by Bush. "That makes two of us. I also like metal— the good stuff, you know?"

"So what do you do after school?"

She sighs and lays down on the bed. "Besides arguing with my sister about my choice to accept the offer to attend here, I study. Here or the library."

I sit on the empty bed against the wall on the other side of the room. I'm surprised she has a room alone but don't point it out. I'm not sure how many people get a scholarship that includes room and board.

"Why doesn't she want you to go here? You told me she grad-uated from here." I turn on my side with my hands tucked under my cheek. "Didn't she get a good job after she graduated?"

"That is the million-dollar question she won't answer."

"She can't or won't?"

"Both."

"Isn't that weird?'

"This place is weird."

While pushing myself upward, I glance out the window and blink briefly as if an eyelash were lodged in my eye. Tall shadows are moving across the concrete. I turn my head to peer out further. The door to the church opens, and three cloaked figures walk out wearing bird masks. I look back at Rose, but she is busy trying to fix her nails.

I look back toward the church, and they're gone. I wipe my eyes with my fingers and blink, but there is no one.

Am I seeing shit?

I look left and right, but it's dark, and the wood door to the church is closed. I lie back on the stripped mattress, looking at the dark wood beams on the ceiling as Bush's "Glycerin" makes way to "If U Think I'm Pretty" by Artemas.

A distinct knock has me sitting up. Rose glances at me, and from the expression on her face, I know she isn't expecting anyone.

I open the door, but there is no one. I take a step and stumble over a large leather-bound book on the floor, resting against the chipped paint of the door. It is a worn leather-bound book.

I pick it up. "What is that?" Rose asks curiously.

I turn the thick leather book over. The cover has no title or author's name, simply the faint smell of ancient parchment and the weight of history.

Rose peers one last time out her door and then closes it. "Assholes. Whoever it was left it for us to find."

"Yeah," I say, taking a seat next to her on the bed.

My curiosity prompts me to touch the worn edge of the book. "Open it."

I cautiously open it, uncovering pages covered with worn writing and forbidden rituals of flesh. The words leap off the pages with powerful impact, capturing my attention. One word jumps out from the title.

"Prey."

The single word hangs in the air, heavy with the weight of

forbidden knowledge. Rose reads along with me. Her eyes move across the pages in sync.

With trembling hands, I trace the lines of text, each sentence unraveling the dark tapestry of the Kenyan University's past. It talks about secret societies, hidden rituals, and a chilling truth buried beneath the veneer of academic prestige.

A cold chill races over my arm, causing my fingertips to shake slightly. My heart quickens with each revelation as we read.

"Oh. Fuck," Rose whispers.

The underprivileged are pawns in a sinister game. They are the Prey, hunted by the privileged elite for sport; their lives are mere playthings to satisfy the whims of the powerful. To be chosen meant to be hunted, to be pursued through the halls and dimly lit corridors, until the predator claimed their prize. Prey are the property of the elite member the minute they accept the offer. A signature binding the agreement is in blood. No one leaves until they are claimed. Once claimed, the predator decides their fate.

I delve deeper into the pages, my stomach dropping with the weight of each revelation. Every minute is a crossroad, a choice looming like a phantom in the night. To turn away meant ignorance, to remain blissfully unaware of the dangers lurking. But to embrace the truth means to risk everything—safety, sanity, and your very soul.

"If a predator claims the hunted and the Prey chooses to stay, the Prey belongs to the predator and is immune to sins of the flesh otherwise forbidden."

"This has to be a joke," she says in disbelief.

I look up at Rose's stricken expression. "It's why your sister didn't want you here. She was..."

"Prey. She was Garret's."

"It's why the sons are married."

"What?" she asks, confused.

I lick my dry lips. "The sons of Kenyan are all married. I bet there is some rule." I flip through the pages. "As a rule, they have to marry before the hunt is over or they graduate. It makes sense. It's why they are all married. It's why they are all close in age. The timing. The scholarships."

It makes sense. It means Valen.

There are no innocents with privileges here, only predators and Prey. Deep down, I could no longer hide in the safety of ignorance. *Reason, not the whims of fate, had chosen them.* I turn the page. And now, Prey must choose—or the choice will be made.

"We're Prey," she whispers, the weight of the truth sinking in.

I nod. "Whoever left this"—I close the book—"is trying to tell us why we are here."

"Why would they...?" She shakes her head slowly, her eyes wide.

"At least we know why they don't have a football team."

They want us to know. They're watching us.

"Wait, wait, wait," Rose says, like something just dawned. "If the rich hunt for Prey, it means they are watching us. They know where we are, right?"

She's right. Like right now, they know we're here. The feeling when I walk on campus. The strange, knowing looks. The leers. That deep feeling I get when people stare at me like they know something I don't. Why my internal alarm went off the first day I walked on campus.

The worst part is that my brother has no idea what he got me into. There is no way he would have allowed me to set foot in this place if he thought I was in danger. A sense of dread rakes over my skin when I think about the night in Valen's pool. The night he said, *"You're mine, now."*

"Have you been with anyone on campus, Rose?"

"No."

"Are you..."

"A virgin? No. I slept with two guys in high school at a party. It's how I learned what assholes they can be once they get what they want."

"This is not high school, Rose. I don't think the people who run this place play high school games."

"Trust me, I think my sister quickly found out. It's probably why she left and didn't look back."

"And it's why you need to stay away from Garret. He's one of them."

"I don't think it's that simple."

"It is. Don't fuck the students who go here." I look out the window at the moon in the sky between the branches of the trees. "If they say they like you or you're pretty, it's a lie. This is a game to them."

"What are you going to do?"

"I'm sure you can't withdraw without owing your life. It wouldn't be that easy once you agreed to come here and then wanted to leave. The only way to survive in this situation is to play their game. Fuck or be fucked." I get up and drop the thick, leather-bound book on her desk with a thud. "And I'm tired of being fucked with."

CHAPTER TWENTY ONE

MELODY

AFTER CLASS THE NEXT DAY, I'm seated at a table in Babylon. It's pointless to hide or return to the trailer where he can find me. If he shows up, which he is bound to do, he will never think to find me here. Waiting. Watching. It's not what Prey usually do. The Prey never becomes the predator. It's usually the other way around, and I've been preyed on before. I've been hunted by their kind. In the past, I was a victim of my own ignorance. Now, it's their stupidity to think I'm a victim.

I ordered the same thing. French fries and water. It is the most I can afford. I haven't told Mr. Crosby I quit the hardware store, afraid he will raise the rent. I was trying to buy myself some time to come up with more money before he found out.

I watch people trying to pick out the players versus the non-players. Basically, predator versus prey. I have come to the conclusion that all the guys are part of the predator club play pool. The girls and guys watching are all prey. Some girls are part of the predator club, but you can pick them out a mile away with their flashy designer handbags and clothes. All students that stay in the dorms are Prey.

"Is this seat taken?"

Melissa takes a seat across from me. Her glossy red lips over straight white teeth. Blond hair that spills around her shoulders. If you want to know what evil looks like, just look at Melissa, and you'll find it. Her smile reminds me of the mother in the movie *Evil Dead Rising*. The expectation is for a woman to embody goodness. Motherly, even, but not Melissa. You can tell everything she does has malicious intent.

There is something about her I don't like, and it has nothing to do with the jealousy licking my gut from the way Valen chose her over me. It's obvious they have something going on. I don't need an explanation or an excuse to see they have a special agreement. It is bigger than an alliance.

"How's your freshman year? It's an important year," she continues, like I give a fuck about what she has to say. "In my opinion, it's the most important. It's where..." She pauses, and she looks whimsical. "Where you break out of your shell and become an adult. A real grown-up compared to when you were in high school and every feeling was magnified, only to come to college and realize how juvenile it all was."

"Is that how high school was for you, juvenile?"

"In some ways, but the sex with Valen wasn't."

She watches me for a reaction.

"Oh, is this your way to warn me off him? Am I supposed to cry now?"

"Now, why would I do that?"

"Isn't that why you're sitting here?"

"Not really. I like you. I think you're pretty." She laughs to herself. "Weird, isn't it? You expect me to be some jealous girlfriend when all I want to do is get to know you better."

The server places the french fries I ordered on the table, and Melissa helps herself to the ketchup, dips a fry, and places it in her mouth. "Mmm... I forgot how something so simple can taste so good." She closes her eyes like she's eating a delicacy and not a greasy french fry.

I can tell it's all an act. Melissa says I'm pretty, and that could only mean one thing. She's into women, and I'm Prey. It's why she's sitting here, trying to intimidate me. To convince me. Feel me out.

"Have you ever been with a woman before? Or...a man and a woman?" she asks with a flash in her eyes.

"No," I say flatly. "I like big, pierced cocks."

She swallows thickly, almost choking on the french fry, and chuckles. "Oh..." She swallows.

She knows whose cock I'm talking about. If I let her think I've seen it, in her mind, it means I fucked him. I want to know what her deal is.

"So... have you been to any parties off-campus?" she asks, changing the subject.

"No. Why?"

She smiles, but there is a hunger in her eyes when she shrugs. "Oh, I don't know. Being a freshman and all, I thought you would have gone to one by now."

"What year are you?"

"Senior."

But I already knew that.

"How did you know I was a freshman?"

"I've never seen you around before, and you have the same look all freshmen do on campus."

"What look is that?"

"The fresh look."

She means the inexperienced look. The look of Prey. Who are these people?

"What are you majoring in?" I ask, acting like I'm interested.

"I'm majoring in communications."

I feel like someone is watching me lick my skin. I look toward the pool tables and see him leaning over the table to take a shot. He holds a pool stick and fixes his gaze on me. A disapproving expression.

Melissa turns around. "He is so jealous sometimes," she says with a gleam in her eyes, "ever since high school."

"Are you two going out?"

She laughs. "If that is what you want to call it..." She pauses. "I mean, we see other people, but we made a promise to each other once we graduated."

Interesting. He made no mention of a promise or her.

"Funny, I never got that impression, but what do I know? I'm just a freshman. I don't know any better, right?"

I know I'm being snarky. I'm jealous and pissed the fuck off. Why wouldn't he make a promise to a girl like her? She's gorgeous and comes from the same circle as he does. She is also older, and I'm young—too young, even if I'm legally an adult. Once he graduates, he will leave and get married as required, and I still have three years to finish college with these monsters. This is their game, and I'm just a pawn.

"I wouldn't say that. College is where you learn, right?" she says with a smile and looks over to where Valen is fixated on us. She turns around, and her smile falls. "Be careful, Melody. Valen doesn't play by society's rules. It's one of the reasons we have an agreement. Once he sleeps with a girl, he moves on to the next. You know how guys are? This is college. Guys want to screw around and have fun. I think girls should do the same. But, like I said, Valen has no heart and is physically available and emotionally unavailable."

"Except with you."

I really hate this bitch.

"Naturally. I've known him since we were kids, so I understand him."

"Of course you do," I say flatly.

She giggles. "If you've fucked him like you just implied"—she lowers her voice enough that I can still hear her over the music—"you're lucky if he lasts forty-eight hours before he fucks someone else. He comes with his own warning, unless you don't mind sharing him with everyone else on campus. The good thing about him is that he's not clingy, and you don't have to worry about him getting jealous if you hook up with someone else. He couldn't care less once he gets what he wants." I look behind her and meet his hard stare as she continues, "Ask any girl on campus; he's practically fucked them all."

I hate what she is saying, but I believe her. He has a sex addiction. He invited me to a party in the hopes that I would find it amusing to observe others fuck. The night at the pool. She is right. He won't stop until he gets what he wants. And like all the rest, he'll do anything to sleep with me. Like taking me to fancy restaurants and ordering me lunch and dinner. Offering me a room in his house instead of the trailer. Acting like a hero at the diner. He isn't going to save me. He did what he did in the parking lot because of his brother.

I slide out of the booth and drop five dollars on the table. "It was nice chatting with you, Melissa. Thanks for the advice."

She smiles. "Anytime. I love to help a girl out."

There is nothing in her expression that indicates she helps anyone out unless it's for her benefit. Melissa is manipulative and a liar.

"Oh, and be careful. They still haven't caught the killer."

Her smile falls, but I ignore her and glance at Valen before I walk out of the bar and tell myself there is one way to get him to forget I exist: give him what he wants.

I walk across the street to the sidewalk and head toward the parking lot. It's getting late, and I have assignments to complete.

"Are you going to leave without saying goodbye?"

I whirl around, and Valen stands in the middle of the sidewalk with his hands in his pockets.

"It looked like you were busy with your game."

He steps closer. "I would have stopped. What were you talking to Melissa about?"

"Worried that I'll cause a rift between you and your girl?"

He makes a face like he just tasted sour milk. "Girl?"

"Yeah, Melissa."

"What about her?"

"She told me you two have a thing. A promise. I get it. It makes sense. The other day at the quad. The way she showed up just now."

His jaw clenches. "What else did she tell you?"

"That you two have an understanding. It's college, right? You're both having fun, but once it's all over...

"Stay away from her. She's..."

"Why?" I say sarcastically. "Because that would make you a liar? A player?" I scoff. "Look, I think it's best we stay away from each other."

I turn around, but he grips my arm, holding me back. I look down at his hand, then at him. "I'm not a liar. Everything I said and did was real."

I pull my arm free. "I'm not saying that it wasn't. I just know that it's just your way of hooking up with a girl you haven't fucked." He flinches like I've slapped him. "Isn't that what you want? To fuck. Scratch that underlying urge you have lodged in your mind. The one that doesn't mean anything."

"What the fuck did Melissa tell you? Whatever she said, she's lying. She's manipulative..."

I shake my head. "So you haven't fucked almost every girl on campus?"

"Have we?"

"But isn't that why you're here? Because you want to? Isn't that what you've been trying to do? At the pool? In your house? Right now?"

His chest is rising and falling. I watch his throat as he swallows. Melissa may be a vindictive territorial bitch who likes to play games, but she wasn't wrong about some of the things she said.

"What am I?" I press. "Number...eight hundred and fifty-three?"

"I..."

"You know what?" I walk backward. "Don't answer that. You wouldn't be the first asshole to use me for their sick games."

I turn around and hurry to my car because I don't want him to see how much it hurts me that he's no different from Zack and the assholes who hurt me.

CHAPTER TWENTY TWO

VALEN

Valen: Follow her.

I WALK into Babylon and scan the bar until my eyes land on Melissa, who is chatting up some girl.

I walk through the throng of people with beers and mixed drinks in their hands until I reach her, trying not to throttle her in front of everyone.

"We need to talk," I say, gripping her by the arm.

"Valen," she protests. Her eyes are wide. "What?"

I push her against the wall in a dark corner. "What the fuck do you think you're doing?"

Her mouth opens and stays stuck for a split second before forming a wicked smile. "So you do like her. How cute."

"What did you say to her?"

"A little of this. A little of that."

I slam my hand against the wall, causing a few curious stares, but I don't give a fuck. "What's your fucking problem, Melissa?"

She slides her pointed, manicured nail down my shirt, and it feels like acid is being poured over my chest. I can't stand her touch, smell, or hell, her fucking voice. If I hated a woman on this earth, it's this bitch right here. She's evil in ways no one can fathom.

The devil himself was present when they created Melissa.

Her laughter grates on my nerves. "You get so worked up over this girl. I never thought you liked the young ones."

"I promised her brother I would keep an eye on her."

"Keep telling yourself that. She told me..." She knows she's getting to me.

"Told you what?" I growl.

What did you say, Melody? Fuck. Telling Melissa anything is like telling the devil all of God's plans.

"That you fucked." My stomach sinks, and my heart sings at the same time. "Well, she mentioned she liked pierced cocks after we mentioned you, and I can only imagine if she said that, you two..." She sticks her tongue in her cheek and jerks her hand in a fist, making a lewd gesture. "That you fucked." She presses her small breasts against my chest, trying to get me worked up but failing miserably. Push-up bras with extra padding should be banned.

I smirk. "What's wrong, Melissa?" I lower my voice and lean close to her ear.

"Does it bother you that I want to fuck the freshman again?" I goad her with my words. "How much I like her sweet, tight pussy. It's so good." My nose inches from her skin by her ear.

Her nostrils flare.

Anyone looking at us this way might think we are having a moment. Maybe it looks like I'm feeling her up in the corner by the bar. I may have a sex addiction, but my cock has its limits when it comes to Melissa, and she fails to do it for me.

My cock has been in hibernation for other pussy since Melody showed up. I swear, I have blisters on the palm of my hand. I haven't jerked off this much since I was thirteen. I saw cum shoot from the head of my cock like a geyser and thought I witnessed a miracle.

With a menacing glare, I lower my voice to a dangerous whisper. "If you hurt her or if I find out you touched her, I'll kill you," I threaten.

The color drains from Melissa's face, and I release her, storming away before she can utter another word. She knows better than to push me further.

I walk back toward the back and spot a familiar face. It's the girl Garret kept eye-fucking the last time Melody was here. She gives me a look of disgust. I don't know what I've done to her.

She's Prey, and it makes sense that she knows Melody. She looks behind me and then back.

Fuck.

She saw me with Melissa, and it looked bad.

Garret meets me out back and says, "She hates you like she hates me."

He's talking about Melody's friend.

"Why would she hate me?"

"It looked like you were practically fucking Melissa in a dark corner by the bar. It doesn't take a genius to know Melody likes you. Rose is her friend. Prey. You know, freshmen link up. Same classes. Like Gia and Jess did when Gia arrived. She saw you."

"It wasn't what it looked like."

"Look, Melissa is a conniving bitch. We all know that, but you're marrying her. It wouldn't be a surprise if you were…"

I unlock my car. "I'm not fucking Melissa."

"Then what were…"

"I was warning her to stay away from Melody."

"So you do like her more than normal."

"She's Adam's sister, and Veronica used to babysit her."

"She's too young for you."

"She's an adult, and I should say the same for you when it comes to Rose. Don't think I didn't see you eye-fucking her while pretending to play pool." I open the door and then remember something. "Didn't you fuck her sister?"

"I wasn't eye-fucking her, and that is none of your business."

"Trying to keep it in the family. That's messed up. But who am I to judge?"

"Says the guy who's fucked half the chicks at school. Scratch that. The school and the chicks at Ohio State."

He makes me feel like I'm a monster, but I hate that he isn't wrong. The first step to a problem is admitting you have one, and I do. I'm just not sure if it's a problem in general anymore or if it has turned into an obsession over one particular girl.

"I haven't—" I begin to protest.

"Lately," Garret interrupts, leaning casually against his sports car.

The back door of Babylon swings open, and Rose emerges, wearing an expression that could curdle milk.

"What's up with the face, Rose? Bad day torturing people," Garret teases.

"Why? Do you want to be next?" she retorts sharply.

"I can find plenty of ways you can torture me... ways you might like," Garret taunts.

She walks up to him and gives him a scrutinizing once-over. I like her. She reminds me of the type of girl who doesn't put up with shit. The kind of girl Melody was when I first saw her. But where Rose's eyes shine with a sardonic brilliance aimed at Garret, Melody's holds a pain. It is a pain that reminds me of Jess when I first met her.

When I look at the pain in Melody's eyes, it releases the evil I hide behind every joke and smile. Darkness no one sees coming.

CHAPTER TWENTY THREE

MELODY

AFTER CLASS, instead of the quad, I find myself inside the library on campus. After Rose sent me the picture of Valen with Melissa at the bar, I knew I needed to stay away from him as much as I could. It meant not going anywhere where I might run into him. It meant avoiding him in every possible way.

I knew he wouldn't stop bothering me. He wasn't going to stop trying because that is human nature. To want something you haven't had is only made worse if you know you can't have it. I'm not trying to play hard to get or anything. I'm trying to get over him. Get over the attraction and the way he makes me feel.

I don't have much experience with guys, and the experience I do have isn't great. I thought of dropping out of school and moving somewhere. Away from my parents' judgment and start over. But it's easier said than done. I went to the financial aid office early this morning, and they said what I assumed. What I feared. I would owe them eighty thousand dollars, even if I supposedly had a scholarship. Some crap about my spot could have been given to someone else.

I looked at the lady behind the computer, wanting to punch her in the face because I knew it meant that they couldn't give it to another underprivileged student the rich assholes couldn't play a game with. This is how they strong-armed you into staying. The trap they set is to make sure you don't leave.

I look at the wood-carved gargoyles on the corner of each aisle and wonder how old this place really is.

My thoughts are interrupted. "Hey, is anyone sitting here?"

A guy with dark hair and darker eyes wearing a Kenyan black

hoodie that reads Swim or Drown is staring at me, waiting for me to respond.

"No," I say, gesturing to the seat in front of me.

He smiles and takes a seat, taking out a history book and notebook. "You're Melody, right?" he asks.

Surprised, I nod. "How do you...?"

"I saw you sitting with Garret and Valen by the courtyard once. My name is Jeremy, by the way."

I pointed at his sweater. "You're on the swim team."

He nods. "Yeah. I'm a junior."

"Freshman."

He smiles. "I know."

"Who..."

"Doesn't? It's not like you can hang around the most popular guy at school, and it doesn't get around or get people talking."

"It's not." I pause. I thought the dead kid found sitting by the tree was a topic. They haven't found out who did it. It's all over the news, but I don't bring it up.

He opens his book and then his notebook. "I'm not judging. All the girls fall for Valen. He has a way to draw girls into his orbit." He snorts. "I thought he could get you at first, but you quickly proved me wrong."

"What is that supposed to mean?"

"Trust me, it's a compliment. It means..."

"What are you doing?" I look up, and Garret is looking at Jeremy like he wants to cut his head off.

"We're studying," Jeremy says slowly, but the tension thickens.

Garret glances at me, his expression inscrutable, and then glares at Jeremy. His voice sinks to a whisper, "You know exactly what I'm talking about."

Jeremy smirks. "What am I doing, Garret? Is there a problem?" he presses.

What is Garret's problem? Am I missing something?

Garret goes quiet, and they have a quiet stare off.

"Is everything alright?" I ask, raising my voice above a whisper.

Jeremy glances at me. "Everything is fine," he says unconvincingly. "I think Garret is under the impression that it's wrong for me to sit here with you." He looks at Garret. "I'm not breaking any rules."

I look up. Rules?

You're Prey, Melody.

The picture of Valen and Melissa is fresh in my mind. It's a game. What he said about me and Valen. He knows I didn't sleep with Valen. These guys know each other better than anyone. In everyone's eyes, or who was at Babylon last night, saw the same thing, or rumors are flying around campus. Valen moved on from the new girl. Me being alone in the library instead of the quad solidified it.

"What kind of rules?"

I know what they are talking about, but I need to play dumb. The way they expect me to be oblivious.

Jeremy smiles but doesn't look at me and says, "It's a team thing. We respect each other's girls." He picks up his pen. "And... last time I checked or from what I heard, you're not with any of the guys on the team."

I place a strand of hair behind my ear. "I'm not," I admit.

Garret glances at me with a solemn look. "Melody..." Garret pauses. "Be careful," he says cryptically before walking away.

I watch him leave the library. "What was that all about?" I ask.

Jeremy looks up. "I don't know. Maybe he thinks I'm going to hurt you or something. I'm not. I'm really a nice guy."

I snort. "Are you?"

"Why don't you find out?"

Jeremy is cute, but I know the game he's playing.

"Where are you from?"

"Upstate Ohio. My parents are lawyers."

"What kind?"

"The expensive kind."

"Let me guess, like most of the rich guys who come here, they want you to be a lawyer and take over."

He smiles. "Not really. I already own a percentage of the firm, and I don't have to be a lawyer. They took care of that part."

"Then why are you in college?"

His grin widens. "Because I'm bored, Melody," he says, going back to the book and flipping a page. "It would look bad if I didn't have a degree when I own a seven hundred-million-dollar law firm at my age."

"What kind of law firm is that? The kind that only hires graduates from Harvard. Like in the show *Suits*?"

He snorts. "No, the kind that shows results. Some are from Harvard; others are from Stanford and Cambridge. You can't have all your eggs in one basket. It would limit potential."

"What basket are you hatched from?"

He knows I'm asking what kind of lawyers his parents are.

"The kind that holds money, power, and influence. The kind that can send their kids to college and get a degree in basket weaving, and it wouldn't make a difference because where there is money, there is lineage. Graduating from Kenyan is enough. You have been given an opportunity of a lifetime."

"It doesn't seem like it."

"That's because you've been hanging around the wrong people."

"And you're better?" I say mordantly.

Jeremy is challenging and infuriating. He should go to law school and become a lawyer. He's got teeth and persuasion.

"I never said I'm the best or better. But I am interesting."

"Aren't you cocky? So you're saying you're better than Valen?" I challenge.

His left eye twitches. I've struck a nerve. "I'm not saying that. If you want to compare, you'll have to hang out with me and be the judge."

I grin. "Is this how you ask a girl out?"

"No." He smiles, and there is a twinkle in his eyes that I don't trust. He writes something down in his notebook, tears the paper, and hands it to me.

I take it, and it reads:.

There are ears everywhere here. I think you're gorgeous, Melody. A guy like Valen doesn't deserve you, and I think deep down you know it. Will you come to my next swim meet?

I write down five simple words and hand him the paper.

If you tell me why,?

He looks around nervously, like he will get caught in class for passing notes. He writes something down and slides the paper over.

My ex-girlfriend cheated on me. She slept with him at a party. Her name is Stephanie. Ask around if you don't believe me. I'm not interested in a girl who wants a guy like that.

What a bitch, and Valen is an asshole for doing it. I can't believe Jeremy wants to use me.

"I know what you're thinking," he blurts. "It's not to get back at anyone. I don't..."

"Want the same thing to happen again?" I finish for him. "And you think..."

I don't have to finish. I can tell by the look in his eyes that he thinks I'm different because I haven't slept with him. I don't think girls recover that easily. I got a taste, and look at me, hiding in the library. I shouldn't hide. It makes me look weak. Vulnerable.

"Alright, I'll go."

"Really?" he asks, surprised.

"Yeah, it's not a date or anything." His smile falls. "I don't date, Jeremy."

"Oh...that's cool. All about school, huh?"

"Yeah."

He shrugs, but I can tell he's bothered. He's good-looking, and he knows it.

Another time, I would have been flattered. Giddy with excitement. I'm just not that girl anymore.

IT'S FRIDAY, and the air crackles with anticipation at the Kenyan swim meet. The scent of chlorine wafts through the venue as I navigate the crowded stands, my heart pounding with a mix of excitement and apprehension. I look around and see a couple of girls from my classes gawking at the guys with their hard abs. They all have perfect physiques without an ounce of fat on their sculpted bodies. I didn't think all the guys on the swim team looked like this under their clothes. I thought it was just Valen. Some have tattoos, but all have smooth skin. The guys from our school wear black shorts like a second skin molded to strong thighs instead of briefs.

"Oh my God..." someone blurts it out.

"He is so fucking hot," the girl below me says, seated next to three other girls wearing skirts so short that it looks like they are sitting in just their panties.

I look up to see who they are talking about, and I'm not surprised. Valen is walking toward the bench with the rest of the guys ahead of Garret and Jeremy. My eyes fall to the bulge between his legs, remembering what his cock looks like underneath. Memories of that night at the pool play in my head, then the picture Rose took of him and Melissa at the bar the other night.

I tear my gaze away and meet dark eyes and a warm smile. Jeremy stares in my direction. I look behind me and find the seat empty. I turn my head, and his smile deepens. He waves at me, and my cheeks heat. There is a thickness in the air, making it hard for me to breathe.

I look a little to Jeremy's left, and hazel eyes meet mine. My smile vanishes, and I look away.

I glance at Jeremy again, but he doesn't look worried. He looks happy. Satisfied. I slide my hands under my thighs to keep them from shaking, trying to avoid looking at Valen, but I can't. Valen makes sure he sits next to Jeremy. His eyes are aimed my way, not paying attention to whatever Garret is telling him. I can see his lips moving, but I can't make out what he's saying.

The girls keep whispering and giggling, thinking he is interested in them, but I know he isn't. Not with the way he is staring right at me. Valen looks pissed.

He asked me that night at the pool to see him swim, and I never did. He knows I'm not here for him.

After a minute, he turns and glares at Jeremy. I don't get why he's mad. He obviously chose Melissa over me. Whatever relationship they had is far from over.

I slide my phone out and pull up the picture Rose sent of Valen and Melissa. His mouth was close to hers like he was about to kiss her. His hand was over her head, flat against the wall, caging her in. Her finger was on his chest. It is clear what they are into with each other. I didn't give him what he wanted, and she obviously was making a point by talking to me about him. It feels like a bunch of needles poke my throat. I hate that every guy I'm attracted to treats me like shit. They think I'm weak and stupid. I look at the picture and forward it to the last number Valen texted me from. I don't have to write anything. The picture says everything I need to say.

He's a manipulative liar.

CHAPTER TWENTY FOUR

VALEN

I WALK into the locker room, pissed off. I won, and I should be happy. I kicked ass and beat my lap time, but it was most likely due to the anger boiling in my veins under the surface. Not even the pool could extinguish it. I pushed myself harder and harder. All I could think about was drowning Jeremy in the fucking deep end of the pool.

I saw the way he looked at her. He invited her, and she accepted. She was there because of him.

I slam my locker, grabbing my towel and glaring at Jeremy. He knows not to look my way, or he'll end up like the last asshole.

I hang my towel and turn on the shower until the water is scalding, not caring if my skin will melt off. I want pain, or I'm going to kill Jeremy in the fucking shower like an inmate in a jail cell.

"I warned him," Garret says, walking in the shower stall to my right. "He said he wasn't breaking the rules."

I wipe the water from my eyes. "Oh yeah..."

Garret isn't helping, but there isn't much he can do when the girl I want won't look at me. She won't answer my calls and is obviously avoiding me at school and making new friends. Friends who are on the swim team and closer to her age with a fat bank account and obsessive tendencies. The last girl he went out with, I fucked, but that was beside the point. She dated him, but she complained that he was stalking her and was obsessive. I'm not far off the scale when it comes to Melody, but he's the weird stalker type. The kind that won't back off if you're not interested. That's why his parents sent him here. It wasn't so he could become a doctor. He can't go to a fancy law school, or it would draw attention if a girl went missing or someone brought a case against him. All that does is tarnish his family name and disrupt the Order.

His being here is what parents do to their offspring who can't make it in normal society after high school or during college. Guys like Jeremy need special treatment, and this is the way to cover up his transgressions until it's time for him to take over his family's legacy.

"Yeah, he said he wasn't breaking any rules."

He's breaking my rules, but I don't tell him that.

"Who said he wasn't?"

"Let it go, man. You can't get all worked up over this. She's single, and technically, you're not."

"Just because the girl you like hates you doesn't mean you get to stick your dick in my soup."

"It's rain on your parade. It's kind of weird talking about dick when we're in the shower."

"The fact that you pointed it out says a lot, Garret. It's okay if you've got a small dick."

He looks down at his cock. "It's not small."

"Yeah, whatever."

I haven't looked and don't plan to, but the whole Victoria Jess thing fucked up his insecurity.

"Hey, guys."

I rub soap on my body, keeping me from punching Jeremy in his smug face. If he touches her, I'll kill him. His parents wouldn't be able to prosecute anyone because I'd cut him up in pieces, and no one would ever be able to find him. It's all I could think about when he was staring at her like a lovestruck fool and waving at her like an idiot. She is oblivious to the danger of accepting anything that has to do with him. As much as there is a fire inside that no one can see but me, there is an innocence about her that drives me wild.

Jeremy walks to the far end of the showers. Neither I nor Garret acknowledge him. Garret doesn't like him, and in my eyes, he's an annoying fly buzzing around that I want to kill. He knows not to provoke me. If she's oblivious to what he is capable of, he's oblivious to what I'm capable of when it comes to her.

Garret shuts the water off and grabs his towel. I wait and do the same thing. Garret gets everyone out of the locker room, locks the door, and shuts off the lights.

"Hey, I'm still in here," Jeremy calls out.

I wait in the shadows until he emerges, his towel wrapped around him. A string of curses echoes off the walls.

"What the fuck?" Jeremy says, annoyed. "You fuckers need to grow up."

I hear his footsteps as he walks toward the exit so he can flick on the lights. I wait until I can get behind him. He doesn't hear me when I wrap my arm around his neck and cover his mouth so he can't scream.

"This is your only warning," I say in a hushed whisper. "Stay away from Melody."

He tries to say something, but his voice is muffled. I squeeze my forearm over his throat, cutting off his air so he gets the point. He struggles, trying to shake me off him, but he can't. I'm stronger and taller. The rage inside me won't abate. It feeds off his weakness and my desire to kill anyone who could hurt her. After a few minutes, he stops struggling, and I put him to sleep, letting his body fall on the wet floor.

Garret turns on the light, and his eyes fall to the body on the floor with no remorse in his expression. The past two years have made him harder. Colder.

"Is he dead?"

I shake my head. "No. I don't feel like cleaning up, and she will know it was me. It's not the right time."

"Alright, let's go."

I check my phone, and there is a text message from her. I grab my stuff, head to the parking lot, and sit in my car so I can open it without Garret around.

I open the message and see it's a picture. I wait anxiously as the picture downloads as I turn on my car. I almost drop my phone the same way my stomach drops and my vision blurs. How? I close my eyes, wondering how she got the picture. I replayed everything that night and know who it was, and I can't blame her for it. She is her friend. Rose saw me with Melissa, and it looked bad, but in Melody's eyes, Melissa was telling the truth. It's why Melissa played into it. She wanted it to look the way it did. She must have known Rose was in there watching. I was too busy threatening her and didn't notice she was playing me, so I would react and use it against me. She wants Melody to hate me to make sure I marry her.

It would make sense for me to tell her father the truth, but that wouldn't benefit me. He would make sure I married her to save face in front of the Order that his only daughter is a lesbian. There is no rule against being gay in the Order, but marriage and lineage between man and woman are requirements. What happens behind closed doors, no one gives a shit about.

Valen: I'm coming for you.

CHAPTER TWENTY FIVE

MELODY

I SLIDE my phone inside my apron pocket, reading the text Valen sent for the fifth time. I scan the booths looking for him, but all I see are Ohio and Kenyan students hanging out and some leaving.

For the past hour, more students have come together. Some leave other groups. I've had to keep tabs on all the checks to avoid someone leaving without paying since it comes out of my pay.

I know Dorothy would let it slide because she knows I need the money, but still, it's my job to keep tabs on checks and orders.

The bell dings, letting me know the food is ready from the kitchen. Tonight, we are swamped. My feet throb, but I'm making tonight what I made a whole week at the hardware store. My last check was for two months' pay, and I know it was Valen giving me money. I almost didn't take it, but I can't afford not to know about the possibility of Zack and his asshole friends telling everyone not to tip me when they come to eat at the diner.

It gets louder. When I turn around, my heart begins to race as my fear slams right into my line of sight. Zack and his friends walk in, taking a seat at the booth of girls I'm about to serve.

I take a deep breath and head over with my head held high even though inside I'm screaming from the nightmare. I can't seem to remember the night they raped me. I place the plates in front of the four girls, ignoring Zack's stare.

"Back again," Zack says playfully. "I knew you couldn't stay away." He reaches into his pocket and places a stack of twenties on the table.

I look up.

He smiles. "For all the times you didn't get a tip. I didn't know you moved out of your parents' house."

I ignore the money and glance at the other girls and his other two friends.

"Can I get you anything else?"

"A thank you would be nice, as would a date Saturday night," Zack says with confidence.

I glare at him like he's lost his fucking mind. "No, and you should put that money away."

I look back at the girls, and then a naughty smile appears over the one with blond hair. "Hi," she says.

It takes me a moment to realize she is not talking to me but someone behind me. I feel him before I can even turn to look at him. He rests his hand on my shoulder. I look over and meet Valen's gaze, full of determination. I try to shrug it off, but he brazenly slides his hand slowly over my ribs and stops at my hips. I can feel the heat through my uniform. Zack and his friend have both eyebrows raised.

"Are you ready?" Valen says, his breath fanning my neck. "I'm so hungry." I can see from the corner of my eye that his gaze is traveling over me suggestively.

"Find a booth, and I'll be right there."

"You're fucking him?" Zack asks, staring right at me.

"I don't blame you," the girl with dark hair says, and then looks at Valen. "We had some good times last semester."

"I'm sorry," Valen says. "Who are you?"

"Party? Last semester. Ohio State won against Penn State. We hooked up at the after-party. I'm Deborah."

"I don't know who you are, Deborah. I was loaded."

"Loaded?" she asks, confused.

"Yeah. I was coked the fuck out. I was going through shit, and I wouldn't have remembered what time it was. I've never seen you before."

Her smile falls when she realizes he's serious. That night was the night. I remember it because of the game. If Valen was loaded, that would mean he didn't know I was there. Zack's gaze shifts from me to Valen, then to Deborah, then to his friend, then to his other friend, before returning to Valen with a worried expression in his eyes.

"You were at the party?" Zack asks, surprised.

Zack didn't know Valen was there.

"Yeah, man. I was there, but I don't remember shit. I had Garret pick me up at around one a.m. I couldn't see straight. I was drunk, high, and drinking Coke. I wasn't in the right headspace. I went into a room that was spinning and got the fuck out. If Garret hadn't called me, I would've passed out. I don't party like that anymore."

"Oh... I never saw you there," Zack says with a look of relief. "Melody was there, though. I guess you really were loaded or would have recognized her."

I feel his hand tighten on my hip. "Oh yeah. Why is that?"

"Oh...yeah. It doesn't matter." Zack glances at me. "Melody had a few drinks, and I had to take her home that night. I was surprised you were there at all. She doesn't remember much either."

Liar. I hate him, and I never thought of seriously hurting someone until Zack and his friends. I drop the pen in my hands and notice they are shaking. Zack raped me. He raped me while I was with his friends.

I bend over, pick up the pen, and practically run to the back of the diner. I check my phone, grateful that my shift is over. I clock out and run out the back, where I find Valen leaning on my piece of shit car.

"In a hurry?" he asks.

"I need to go," I say in a shaky voice.

"Do you always cry when you see your ex?"

I swipe my face and notice my hands are wet. I'm crying.

"Leave me alone, Valen."

"We both know that's not going to happen. What's wrong?"

He isn't going to let this go. He's going to keep meddling until he gets what he wants.

He can't save me.

He can't change the past.

I walk up to him, defeated. His eyes fall to my face. I summon the inner me. The one that I locked away after that night. I need to let that version of me loose. There is only one way he will leave me alone so I don't lose myself entirely. I can use this as an experiment. A way to fix myself for when the right person in my life comes along.

That person doesn't deserve a broken girl. That man deserves the old me. The one with a smile and who is not afraid of life. The Melody who wasn't afraid to try new things. Have dirty sex. The Melody who wanted to fall in love. How could I ever expect to fall in love when I'm afraid of a man's touch?

I knew I was raped. I felt sore and violated. I got checked out at the free clinic, and I was relieved that I was okay. I didn't catch anything, but the damage was done. The fear of a man's touch was embedded in my skin. In my mind. What if I cried out when the guy I like touched me?

I step closer, leaving a small space between us, and look up. "I want you to fuck me."

He raises a brow. "Prove it."

I reach between his legs and grab his cock over his sweats, feeling it grow hard in my hand. I feel the barbells between my fingers.

"Fuck me."

"Why?"

"You said to prove it. I'm doing what you asked."

"Why the change of heart? What are you trying to prove?"

"I'm asking you for sex. Are you saying no?"

My chest squeezes. This is not going as I planned. He was supposed to be excited and take me to the nearest wall, hike up my skirt, and fuck me. Not interrogate me.

"I'm not saying that. I'm asking you why you want me to fuck you. You're not asking to make love or have sex. You said fuck."

"Do you know how to make love, Valen?"

"I'm not the kind who does, Melody. I'm the kind who makes you beg for more." He lowers his voice. "I'm the kind who fucks you in a dark corner while other people are unaware that you're getting fucked...hard."

"Like at the bar?" I fire back.

"I didn't fuck her. She wished I would, but I won't. I can't."

"Why?"

"Because there is a freshman I'm dying to fuck and make her mine, but she thinks I don't want her."

"What do you want?"

He grips my throat, eliciting a gasp. His eyes turn pitch black. "Whatever it is, you are willing to give me."

We stare at each other for a few seconds at the darkness inside us. His eyes were promising pain, pleasure, danger, and titillation. Mine promises the minefield of my worst nightmare and the girl I used to be. The one who would be face down on the back seat of my car with my ass in the air while he fucked me, begging me to be quiet.

"What do you want the most?" I ask.

"I want your fear," he says.

All I can think about is the fact that sometimes rebirth requires the death of the soul.

"Is that all?"

"I want your consent. I won't ask for it again once you agree."

"Condoms."

He grins. "Condoms," he mocks. "I don't have anything, but if it's pregnancy you're worried about..."

"It's not that. It's..."

"You think I'll sleep around."

"You don't owe me."

"I'm not going to fuck anyone else, and I'll give you peace of mind."

I drag my hands away from him reluctantly. "Like?"

He laces his fingers with mine. "Proof that I'm clean, and I need you to know that I have a dirty appetite, Melody. Right now, I'm like a caged animal."

"I'm your Prey, right?"

He smiles, but his eyes tell me he's surprised that I know that term and what it means.

"Since you set foot in Kenyan. I marked you. You're mine."

"I choose until you get bored."

"Who said I was bored?"

Let the games begin.

He removes his hand from my throat and tilts my chin up. The clouds moving over the moon cause the light to make his face appear sinister.

"I'm going to break you, Melody. I'm going to take everything inside you, including your breath, away. I'm going to be your new nightmare."

My fingers play with the band of his sweatpants, feeling his warm, smooth skin underneath.

"Why?"

"I've been waiting for you, Melody. When we first saw each other, there was nothing to say. Our eyes meeting was just enough." He takes my hand so I can feel his hard stomach. The deep grooves that make up his ab muscles. "You're not in high school anymore. You're not underage, but I promised your brother I wouldn't touch you." He smiles and lowers his voice, placing his lips over the lobe of my ear. "I lied." Sharp tingles slide down my neck.

CHAPTER TWENTY SIX

MELODY

I TAKE the last step and turn right down the hallway, not wanting to miss out on getting something to eat. I end up at the vending machine, scanning the choices.

"Hey?"

Jeremy walks up. I know what he wants. For me to answer his calls. After my little agreement with Valen last night, he followed me home to make sure I was safe. Jeremy called me four times and left three text messages. It was a little excessive, but I did leave after Kenyan won and didn't say goodbye.

"Hey," I say, still looking at the chocolate chip cookies.

"I was worried about you last night. I didn't hear from you, and you left after."

I press D9 while watching the machine dispense the pack of cookies. "I had to work." I push the black opener and grab my cookies. "By the time you called, it was late," I say, giving him a weak smile. "Sorry."

He shifts on his feet. "That's okay. I was worried. You know, it's not safe out there."

I walk to the drink machine, find the Dr. Pepper, and slide in three single-dollar bills. "I'm good."

He places his forearm on the edge of the machine, watching me press the button, and asks, "I was wondering if you wanted to hang out?"

"I'm sorry, Jeremy. I don't…"

"Date," he finishes for me. "Right, but it wouldn't be a date. Just two friends hanging out."

I hate to turn him down. He seems nice, but I know the real reason.

"She doesn't need friends."

Jeremy looks back at me and straightens. The muscle in his jaw tics. Jeremy hates Valen.

The sound of the can dispensing like a bowling ball as it makes its way out breaks the silence. Valen bends and grabs the soda can.

"She can be the judge of that, but I'm surprised you care. I thought you would be fucking Stephanie somewhere."

Jeremy is obviously not over his girl cheating. I think he needs some time to get over her. I know what it feels like to be cheated on, and it sucks. I'm no expert, but he needs to be careful. I wouldn't provoke Valen. He looks calm, but I can sense something dark and ominous changing the air.

"I don't know. You should look for her since you're still hung up on her. I was high and don't remember what she looks like, to be honest. Stephanie is such a common name. In my mind, she could be anyone." Valen glances at me and asks, "What were you doing upstairs?"

"Nothing. I was curious, but the door was locked."

I didn't think anyone saw me. This place is vast, with certain areas designated for specific purposes. I haven't gone to the church and wonder who actually goes inside. The other night in Rose's dorm has been playing in my mind.

"Administration locks it during class hours," Valen says, ignoring that Jeremy is still listening.

"That makes sense. I'm going to head to the library."

"I'll go with you," Jeremy chimes in.

Valen grins. "The library is my favorite place."

When we walk in, it's practically empty, except for the couple in the back. The girls seated in front. I take the table to the far left by the encyclopedias. I place the soda and cookies on the desk, and Jeremy makes a beeline for the seat next to mine like a child wanting to sit in the front.

Valen pulls the chair out for me, which infuriates Jeremy. I think it's amusing how they are fighting over me because I know it's not because I'm gorgeous. It's part of their game. I should act flattered, but Valen would see right through it. So I act like it's normal and happens to me all the time.

After thirty minutes of hard stares between them, I walk to the back of the library, looking for a reference for an assignment.

It's quiet and dark back here.

The fluorescent lights make it hard to see the spines of the books. The one I need is on the last shelf. I try to reach for it— the feel of the cold air on the crease of my ass where my skirt has ridden up. My fingertips graze the leather spine of the book. I'm reaching as far as my arm will go, widening my legs a bit until I can get my fingernail to pull at the spine, so I slide the book out. I managed to get it. I pull the book back and fall to my heels.

Something wet and warm slides over my slit, causing me to gasp. I look down, and Valen is lying face up on the carpeted floor with his face pushed up between my legs.

His fingers grip my thighs, hooking my thong with one finger, and he spreads my lips apart. I look left and right, relieved no one can see what is happening. Heat runs up my neck. Nerves shoot between my thighs. He eats my pussy. I should push him off, but I can't.

It's hot and dirty. His face is wet and glistening. His tongue swipes up the crack in my ass and back to my clit. I ride his face, biting back the moan that wants to slip out.

I grind on his face. Faster and faster. My breathing is heavy. I drop the book and grip the shelf, my knuckles turning white. It feels so good. I grip my skirt in a fist with one hand so I can see his face.

His nose is shoved up in my pussy, and I feel him breathing. His nostrils are flaring with each lick. He fucks me with his tongue for a good five minutes, and when he slides his finger in my ass, I jerk violently as my orgasm slams into me like a gust of wind. I'm shaking, trying to hold on to the shelf to keep my knees from buckling.

"Oh fuck," I whisper when he holds my thighs steady and sucks the cum from my pussy.

When he finishes, I raise my leg to allow him to stand. I try to fix my skirt, remembering that Jeremy is waiting for me at the table, but he grips my chin and kisses me, rubbing his wet face all over my lips. I tasted myself on his tongue. It's sexy, and I want more. I want him.

"Your cunt is so pretty and tight. I'm addicted," he says, placing a soft kiss on my lips and walking away.

I watch him leave through the space between the shelves, not stopping by the table, and walks out of the library.

I make it back to the table, the book forgotten, wet between my legs. Jeremy looks up when I start to collect my things.

"Is everything alright?"

"Yes," I say, trying to hide the flush in my cheeks.

I didn't want him to stop. I wanted to keep going, but there are people. In the heat of the moment, no one existed, but in the back of my mind, I was worried we would get caught. It was a rush I never knew I needed. If he's addicted, I'm obsessed.

"You're leaving?" he asks.

"Yes." I hesitate. "I need to get home. I forgot I had something to do."

"Can we hang out later?" he asks hopefully.

"I'm sorry, Jeremy. I can't."

He lowers his head, but it's better this way. I can't lead him on when I'm not interested. I have to admit, I went to the swim meet because, deep down, I wanted to see Valen. I could tell myself a hundred times I didn't go because of him, but it's a lie. I want Valen. Since the first time I saw him.

I grab the rest of my things. "I'll see you later."

"I'm counting on it," he says before I walk out.

CHAPTER TWENTY SEVEN

MELODY

I HEAR A TAP. I sit up and wince from the stiff muscles on my lower back. I need a thicker mattress to sleep on. Every morning, I feel like someone hit me with a car when I get up.

I look out the little window. The sky is dark. The moon hides behind the thick clouds. The fog is thick. I check my phone, and it's 2 a.m. I just fell asleep an hour ago. All I could think about was Valen and what happened in the library. I couldn't concentrate on the paper I have to write.

I hear it again. *Tap. Tap. Tap.*

I sigh and stand, grabbing a thick sweater that falls to mid-thigh. I slide my feet into my black boots and grab my phone. It must be something the wind dragged, and it's stuck against the side of the trailer, making that stupid tapping noise. If I don't pull it off, I won't get any sleep. I have school in the morning.

I push open the door, tap the flashlight on my home screen, and walk outside. The wind picks up, and I shiver from the cool air. It's getting colder.

All the lights are off in Mr. Crosby's house. He won't be back until Monday. He left to go visit his daughter in Maine.

The trees sway. The sound of an owl breaks the silence. I angle the light and walk around the trailer, looking for a piece of plastic or a piece of debris swaying in the wind and hitting against the wall of the trailer, but I don't see anything. I walk to the backside of the trailer, away from the street, but don't see anything. I glance behind me toward the tree line, a weird feeling snaking up my spine.

I keep walking, raising my phone so the light can shine on top.

Maybe something is stuck by the window, making that annoying sound, but I don't see anything.

A shadow falls against the trailer, and I look to my right. It feels like my heart is stopping. Someone stands wearing a plague mask and a large robe with a hood over their head. It's the same kind I saw from Rose's dorm room window near the church entrance.

I blink a couple of times to see if I'm hallucinating, but I'm not. Whoever it is, they're standing and watching me. The eyes from the mask were pitch black and shiny, reminding me of the button eyes in the movie *Coraline*.

"Who are you?" I ask.

It shakes its head slowly.

I open the app to dial 911 when it comes at me, causing me to drop my phone. I run. I run so fast that the cold air invades my lungs like a whip, not letting me swallow. Not letting me scream for help. I can hear the footsteps gaining behind me. The sounds of feet hitting the ground like a horse.

I push through the branches of the trees, hitting my face. Some snag my hair as I run through the woods, kicking the leaves in my panic. I can feel whoever is behind me. They're close, and I'm tired. I don't run, and I'm not into sports. The air is thinner as I run deeper into the woods. My fatigue grips me in its embrace.

I snag my boot on the root of a tree, and I fall, hitting the wet leaves and dirt. My hair is blinding me when I look up.

Pain grips my skull when I'm thrown back on the ground. Strong thighs pin me to the ground as the man straddles me.

I hit his chest, feeling how hard his body was with each blow, but it's as if they are made of concrete. Every hit I land does nothing to diminish their power over me. Tears burned the backs of my eyes. Please stop.

"Please!" I scream. "Please..."

A gloved hand wraps around my throat and mouth, hindering me from screaming or calling for help. The beak of the mask runs over the skin of my cheek in a caress. I can't move. I try to move my thighs, but I can't. He has me pinned underneath him.

"Let me go," I demand.

He shakes his head and squeezes my throat tight enough so he can remove the hand covering my mouth and slide it up my thighs.

"Don't." The hand stops but then slides between my legs and rips my panties.

Two fingers pinch my clit, causing me to cry out. The trees rustle, and birds fly into the sky.

He pulls something out from under his robe, and I notice it's a ball gag. He swiftly wraps it around my head and shoves it in my mouth. I'm too exhausted to fight. Tears slide down my cheeks. My vision goes in and out. This has to be a dream. If I close my eyes, I'll wake up, and it will be morning, but when I open my eyes, he's between my legs, tying my hands above my head and tying the rope to the root of the tree. The same fucking one I tripped on.

I try to pull my arms free when I feel a surge of adrenaline, but I can't. He knew what he was doing, getting me to run. He wanted me to be tired and without enough strength to fight him off.

He's one of them. I can feel it. There is nothing I can do. He will find me. They will find me.

I can't speak. I can't move. His weight is on my hips, keeping me from kicking out with my legs.

His leather-gloved hands lifted my sweater, grabbing me by the hips. His thumbs are caressing my skin. He dips the beak of his mask, sliding the leather tip over my slit. I moan at how dirty and crazy it feels. My pussy is not in tune with the terrors crossing my mind. He plays with my clit with the tip of the mask.

I moan like I'm on the set of a porn flick. It spurs him on, and he moves faster until I'm shamelessly coming, looking up at the dark sky with tears in my eyes. I'm messed up.

I'm so fucked.

My sweater is shoved ruffly up to my neck, exposing my breasts. The air claws at my heated nipples after he pinches them.

I hear the rustle of fabric and then the feel of something hard between my legs. His cock is hot and heavy right at my entrance, teasing me. I close my eyes and then feel it when he roughly shoves his huge dick inside me. My eyes snap open, and I feel it. I feel him.

He fucks me hard. Savagely. My ass lifts off the ground. His thrusts snatch the air from my lungs. He growls like an animal. One hand grips my throat. My body was wet with sweat. Thick fog rolls in like a tie all around us, but he doesn't let up. Fireworks go off behind my eyes as I feel every inch of his cock.

He grips my legs roughly, spreading them wide as he takes me to the ground. The fog is a backdrop behind the bird mask as he looks at me through the shiny black eyes. He looks frightening. My tits bounce every time he pounds into me.

I can't take it.

I can't hold it anymore, and I come hard.

A strangled moan escapes my throat, muffled by the gag in my mouth, followed by a loud growl from his throat. He comes inside me, and I smile.

I bolted up from the bed, wrapped in a warm blanket. I look around, trying to remember where I am while my eyes try to focus on the sun streaming from the window. I see the dust motes floating above me. I look to my right, and my throat clicks, feeling the soreness of my throat, while my eyes zero in on the bird mask sitting on top of the Formica top.

I shove the blanket off, touch myself, and wince. I'm sore like a freight train was shoved up my insides.

It happened. It was real, but I don't remember when I got home or how.

I look around, but nothing is different except the scratches on my body from the trees and the soreness between my thighs.

THE DOOR behind me shuts with a loud thud in the church. The church is empty. There are four confessional booths to my right. I've never been a religious person, and my parents took me to church to get baptized and complete my confession, but other than that, I haven't set foot inside a church. I don't think I remember confessing my sins.

I walk over to the middle booth, see that the light is on, and then walk inside. The smell of rich wood, candles, and flowers envelops me. I see someone sitting on the other side through the lattice window.

The priest on the other side begins, "In the name of the Father and Son and the Holy Spirit..."

I glance up at the engraved message on the wood.

THEY'RE ALL LIARS. SPILL YOUR SINS SO THEY CAN HEAR YOUR PATH TO HELL.

"Are you with me, my child?" the priest says from the other side.

The words stick in my throat. The words I thought I would say were forgotten. My mind goes blank.

"Are you still with me?"

"Yes."

"Do you remember what needs to be said?"

"Oh, bless me, Father, for I have sinned."

"When was your last confession?"

I close my eyes, trying to remember, but I can't. It's all a blur.

"I don't remember," I say honestly.

"Well, it will come to you. It's something you don't forget easily. It's like driving a car or praying for your sins. You remember that, don't you?"

"Yes, I guess I do."

"Well, what are your sins so you can ask God to forgive?"

"Umm... I had sex last night."

"I see. Out of wedlock, I'm assuming."

"Yes."

"Is the other person married?"

"See, Father. I think I know who he is, but I'm not sure. I don't remember. I thought it was a dream, but it wasn't."

"Who do you think it was?"

I pinch my brows and reply, "How bad is it?"

"Depends on whether it was real or not. If it happened, if it did, you committed a sin of the flesh. Fornication is a sin. If it didn't, and it was all in your mind, it's still a sin, but not as bad. Sometimes the thought of sinning can be placed in a person's mind, but as long as the thoughts don't lead to actions."

This priest is weird. This feels like an interrogation.

He goes quiet for a few seconds. "Is there anything else you want to tell me, Melody?"

A chill runs down my spine.

"I didn't..."

I slide the door to the confessional booth open and run out. I rush out the door and into something hard. I look up and sigh.

"What's wrong?" Valen asks, holding me close.

"I went to confess and..." I swallowed thickly, trying to catch my breath. "He knew my name and asked me things."

"Wait here," he says calmly and walks inside.

I look around and catch the entrance to the cemetery. The tombs look old, like they were here for centuries. I wonder who they have buried there, and why does the school have a cemetery next to a church?

The door to the church opens, and Valen walks down the steps.

"What happened?" I ask.

"Where were you last night?"

"I was home, but you didn't answer my question."

"You don't know."

"What? I'm not following."

He pulls out my phone, and I look at the news article.

ANOTHER OHIO STUDENT DEAD

It says Jacob Macnab was found dead in the woods, four miles from campus. His body was mutilated.

I look up, handing him his phone back. "He plays football."

"He was also at the diner with Zack when you ran out crying. Do you know him?"

"No," I lie, but I think I do.

He was with Zack that night. He said it when that girl claimed to have screwed Valen the same night he said he was loaded. I don't remember how, but I know he was one of them.

"Is there something you need to tell me, Melody? You can trust me, baby. I need you to tell me what you know."

"Where were *you* last night?"

He looks at his phone.

"Home with Azriel finishing school."

My phone vibrates in my back pocket. I take it out and see it's a text from Rose.

Rose: Come to my dorm room.

Melody: See you in five.

"I gotta go. I need to see Rose. What did that crazy priest say?"

"Nothing." He shakes his head and pockets his phone. "He didn't say anything. He was waiting for you to finish and said you ran out like the booth was on fire."

The guy is a liar, but I don't tell him that.

I pocket my phone, and then it goes off from another message.

I pull it back out and open it.

I look up. "I'll meet you outside of Drury Hall in an hour," he says, nodding slowly.

"HEY," Rose greets me when I walk in.

"Did you hear about the Ohio student turning up dead?"

"Yeah, but that's not what I wanted to talk to you about," she says with a slight frown.

"What is it?"

She pulls out her phone, scrolls through it, and hands it to me. "I was looking online through social media and found these. It doesn't make sense because of the dates. I couldn't make sense of it."

I scroll through screen shots of pictures of me at a party, but these are dated three years ago. I was still in high school. I keep scrolling, and I see Madison with me in one of them. I hated that we looked different. We don't look related at all, but I stop scrolling when I see one of Valen and me.

"Where did you get this?" I ask, holding up the phone and pointing at the picture.

"That's why I texted you to come over. Did you know Valen from before?"

I shake my head. "No. I mean, I saw him at a party once when I was still in high school."

I tell her about Zack and why I was there.

"But why does the picture before show you wearing an Ohio State sweater? Based on the dates of these pictures, you should be a senior, not a freshman. It doesn't make sense."

It doesn't. I look through the pictures, and it's me, but not me, if that makes sense. Like I have a doppelgänger.

"Have you shown these to anyone?"

She shakes her head. "Good, don't."

I hand her phone back and open the door.

She looks up with a worried expression. "Where are you going?"

"I'm going to ask the only person who can tell me the truth."

CHAPTER TWENTY EIGHT

VALEN

I EAGERLY WAIT for her to come out of Drury Hall like a caged lion. I can't take this anymore. I miss her. I miss my girl. I know I said an hour. I keep checking the time on my phone to keep me from barging in there and dragging her out so I can take her home, but I can't.

I look up when the door opens, and she walks out. "Valen?"

Fuck, she's gorgeous. I can't get her off my mind. "I'm sorry. I know I said an hour, but I saw you run out of the church, and then I texted you and didn't want you to freak out."

She smiles, and that's her. "Why would I be afraid? You're here."

I walk up to her and kiss her hard and deep.

She pulls away with a laugh. "Are you here to take me home?"

I nod like an idiot because I love to hear her say that. Home.

When I walk inside my house, I don't waste time and drag her to the bedroom. I shove her short skirt up her thighs and tear her pantyhose.

She pulls out my cock and surprises me by dropping to her knees.

She looks up. "I love you," she says for the first time, and my heart breaks.

She takes me inside her mouth, and I close my eyes, feeling her tongue on my cock like the first time I met her. She takes me deep, and I almost come on the spot.

"Fuck!" I growl and grip her hair, fucking her mouth.

She draws me in with her expert mouth. I pull out and push her face down on the bed, grip her thighs, lift her feet off the ground, shove my cock inside her wet, dripping cunt, and fuck her.

"Yes, Valen," she says and then moans. "Mmm...deeper, like last night."

I smile. She remembers.

I fuck her hard, our skin smacking against each other. The bed bangs against the wall with each forceful thrust. I pull her hair, causing her back to arch.

"Are you going to tell me?"

She smiles wide and pushes against me as my cock slides deep. "And ruin all my fun?"

I grin because this version of herself is unpredictable. Powerful. "I love all the parts of you, Melody."

She undulates her hips. "Do you?" she says in a naughty voice.

I squeeze her hips, slowing down. She knows how to make me come. She rolls her hips faster, and a drip of sweat lands on her lower back.

I squeeze my eyes shut, savoring the moment right before I explode inside her. "Fuck, baby," I grunt as hot cum shoots inside her.

When we're done, I clean her up and toss her pantyhose in the trash. She looks at her fingers and pouts.

"Where is my ring?" she asks.

I smile and open the drawer. "You put it in here last night before you went to bed."

I hand her the five-carat pear-shaped solitaire.

She slides it on and smiles. "I did put it there, didn't I?"

"Yeah, you forget sometimes."

She walks up to me naked, except for the giant rock on her finger, and wraps her arms around my neck. "What else do I forget?"

"Your homework. You have a bad habit of forgetting to do it."

She angles her head like she is lost in thought. "But I don't have any." She furrows her brow like she has figured something out. "I graduated, remember?"

"Almost, you have three more classes. The ones you missed, remember. When you were sick."

I try to blink back the sting from my eyes. I hate this part. The part that she won't tell me. The part I have to hide from everyone. The part she won't tell me because it hurts.

"Hmm...is that why I was at the dorm?"

"You were visiting a friend." She giggles. "How come I forget things?"

"Sometimes, we forget things because they remind us of things that happened. There are things that hurt, but we have to remember the things that make us happy."

"You make me happy. Do I forget about you?" She says it in a little voice.

"You can never forget me because I want to fall in love with every part of you." I squeeze her ass and press my hard cock against her belly. "Even the forgetful ones," I say with a smile and whisper, "Let's go to bed."

"Don't we have class?"

"Not today."

I STARE at the tiny picture. My soul is breaking into a million pieces. The pad of my thumb tracing the glossy surface of the black-and-white picture.

"You alright?" Azriel asks. I nod and place it between the pages of the little black book. "How is she?"

"Asleep."

"You're not going to take her back, are you?"

"I can't leave her there. I can't sleep in my car forever. I also can't ask you to keep doing it either, and I don't trust anyone else when it comes to her."

"Does she remember?"

I shake my head. "No, and when something is triggered, another asshole ends up dead."

Azriel smiles. "At least she has help."

"It would help if she would tell me what happened."

"She was looking for you. Well, the other part of her was. Now that I know the truth."

"I'm sorry I didn't tell you. How could I?"

"I get it. I'm not upset, but you could have told me you loved her. It would have all made sense."

"No one knows except you."

"It means a lot, brother. You trust me enough to tell me something that is not easy to admit." He smiles. "I loved that she was doing things like before."

"You mean you got her to watch scary movies again?"

"Hell, yeah. She loves the scary ones. She likes M&Ms in her popcorn, and I made sure to buy all her favorites. I want her to think it was all my idea."

I shake my head. "You're making me jealous."

"Do you think she will be mad if I tell her that I've seen the same movies with her before? I mean..." He pauses. "You know what I mean."

"I want to tell you something important." He looks up. "I have never cheated on Melody."

"Does she know that?"

"I think part of her does. The deep parts, the one that counts, but there is something else I need to tell you. Something no one knows. Not yet."

He gives me his full attention, and I begin.

CHAPTER TWENTY NINE

MELODY

MY EYES FLUTTER OPEN, and I yawn. It feels like I'm floating on a cloud. My throat is a bit sore, and my tongue is stuck on the roof of my mouth, but something is different. My back doesn't hurt, and I'm not in the trailer. I take a deep breath. The familiar smell of citrus and cedar.

I look to my right, to my left, and then at the ceiling. Where am I?

I sit up and notice the expensive furniture. The huge bed I'm in.

I lift the comforter, and I'm naked. My hand snags on a thread from the sheet, and I see a huge diamond ring on my finger. I extend my fingers and see the way the stone glitters in the light coming in from the huge bedroom window.

I glance at the nightstand and notice the picture frame of Valen and me. I don't remember when it was taken. I open the drawer and find two cell phones on a wireless charger. I pick up my phone, then the other. I look at the late-model cell phone, guess the code, and it unlocks.

I notice it mirrors my phone, except there are messages from my sister Madison from yesterday asking how I'm doing. Messages I don't remember sending.

I scroll to Valen's name and open the thread messages.

> Valen: You look beautiful when I'm inside you.

Valen: I love the color of your hair when the sun rises in the morning. I think it's one of my favorite things when I wake up next to you. I hate that there are times when you forget how I feel about you. How do I feel about us?

Melody: I could never forget you. I could never forget us.

Valen: You're my favorite part of my day, Melody. Don't forget to come home to me.

Melody: Always.

The bedroom door opens.

"You're awake."

"Veronica?"

"Of course, it's me." She takes a seat on the bed. "Who did you think would barge in on you and not care if you're naked?"

I remove the sheet and cover myself. "How did I get here?"

She gives me a sympathetic look. "I'll show you." She gets up and opens a drawer, handing me one of Valen's T-shirts. I pulled it over my head. "He loves when you wear his clothes."

I close my eyes, briefly loving the scent of him still clinging to the fabric. When I open my eyes, she places a book on my lap. I sit cross-legged on the bed, and she begins, "You told me to give this to you when the time is right, and I think that time is now."

"What do you mean? It feels like I haven't seen you in forever."

She laughs. "You were with all of us the other day. You don't remember because the Melody that was with us was the older version of you."

She pulls out her phone and shows me a picture of her, Gia, me, and then another one of Jess and three gorgeous kids. There is something wrong. I don't remember going there. I don't remember any of it.

Tears run down my cheeks. "What's wrong with me, Veronica?"

"You have DID, or multiple personality disorder. You have an alter. I'm not an expert, but in a nutshell, you have a younger version of yourself and an older version of yourself. The problem is you don't remember what the younger one does when the older one is present, and vice versa." She hands me a designer wallet. "Open it," she demands.

I open it, and I look at the driver's license and credit cards, all in my name. "I've never seen this before."

"Of course you have. The other you. Look at the date of birth on your driver's license."

I do, and I'm older. The pictures Rose showed me and the one on the nightstand. Veronica is right.

"And Valen?"

"He knows. He's...known."

"The whole time?"

"Yeah, the whole parents' thing and babysitting thing makes sense now that I saw for myself how wild the older version of you was, but something happened."

I sniff. "It did, but I don't remember all of it."

"Tell me what you know before more bodies turn up, or your man decides to kill the entire football team and leaves your brother as the only player on the field."

"It was him?"

"He says it wasn't, but I'm not sure. He would do anything for you. I think it's safe for you to tell me what you know."

I tell her.

When I'm done, my hands are like two balls in my lap, and I'm rocking back and forth.

"He doesn't know, does he?"

I shrug. "I don't know how much he does know."

"He's not friends with them, Melody. He was at those parties because of you, and believe me, the older you are, the more in love you are with Valen."

"And the younger? Me...the one here right now?"

"Are you?"

I look at my hand and see where the diamond is on my finger. "I don't know. The more I read the back-and-forth texts between me and him, the more certain I become. I love him, but there is a doubt. I have a small, lingering doubt, and I don't know why."

"It's because he doesn't know what Zack and whoever was responsible for raping you did. There is something the younger you do not know. It's what the older you are protecting you from. It's the way the mind protects itself."

"Tell me."

"It would change everything, Melody," she says with a pained expression. "It could destroy you, but it could help you all at the same time. Things will click, but he would hate me for it."

"Why?" I am confused.

"He wants the younger you to fall in love with him the way the older you already is."

"The ring."

"I'm going to guess, but that rock on your finger can only mean one thing. One thing that you two share. A big secret."

"Like Azriel."

"Like Azriel."

"We're married, aren't we?"

She grins. "Yes, Melody. As of eight months ago, you are Mrs. Vikiar."

"It's why I'm in Kenyan?" I ask, trying to piece everything together.

"Among other things."

"I'm not a freshman, am I?"

"In your mind right now, yes. Technically, no. You're a senior."

She scrolls through her phone and shows me countless pictures of dates, the restaurant he took me to, and us kissing passionately. The smile on both our faces tells me we are so hopelessly in love with each other.

"What am I protecting myself from?"

The look in her eyes tells me that whatever she is going to tell me will break me.

"You were pregnant, Melody. You lost the baby, and the younger you took over."

I gasp. "When? How?

No, no. How could I? But it's possible. The clinic.

"I think you know, baby."

"How did they..."

Someone knew. They knew I was pregnant.

"Valen knew you were pregnant, and he spiraled. Drugs and alcohol, but he never cheated on you. That I can guarantee. He is so worried about you," she says, and then sobs. "I have never seen him like that." Her voice grows thick with emotion. "He would follow you everywhere. He would hire people. He would ask Garret. I mean, he would let you be you, but he was always there, waiting for you to come back, and when you didn't..."

"When did we start dating?"

"He saw you at the party that night, and then he was obsessed. Then he met the older you. The one Adam was trying to look after at school. Your sister. Your parents. I didn't get it at first, and then they told me the truth. You're adopted, Melody. Your mom abandoned you when you were five, and you showed signs of DID around ten, and then it stuck. Your mind created an altered way to deal with the trauma. It's why you have a hard time remembering, but Valen didn't give a shit. We have our crap. He has his, right? When he saw the older you, I guess you guys had a thing. Then he saw you at the party with Zack, and he was stunned. He was confused, and Adam explained it to him, but you were young. This version of you had to grow up."

"He had to wait."

"Yeah, it was hard for him, but he waited until you were eighteen and swooped right in and made the older you and him official in secret."

"The younger me had to feel the same way."

"I think it's what the doctors said. After the miscarriage, you shut down. You left your parents' and moved to the trailer, and there was nothing no one could do but give you time."

It all makes sense.

"And now?"

"Now you tell him the truth about how you lost the baby before you do something crazy."

"Like what?" I am perplexed.

"Like find another dead kid sitting at a tree with his throat cut." She leans close and lowers her voice. "You didn't think he was there by coincidence, did you?"

"The other one found in the woods?"

She smirks. "Your husband hates to see you cry. He also hates when you work or when an asshole insults you."

The diner. Jacob was at the diner. It means Zack is next, but there is something I'm missing. There is something that doesn't make sense. Why? If they knew the older me was with Valen, why would they drug and rape me?

"Did Zack know about my disorder?"

"I'm sure he did. Why?"

I get up and hastily get dressed. "He was part of it, Veronica. He was there, and I remember another name. Sam. There was a guy named Sam, but I was drugged and was in and out. The fact that the other me doesn't remember what the younger me does doesn't help."

"Tell him, Melody."

"I think he knows, Veronica. It's why I'm here and not at the trailer. It's why you're here suddenly, talking to me about this."

She smiles. "He did say you were smart as fuck."

CHAPTER THIRTY

VALEN

TAKING a seat in front of the other members of the Order and Consortium, I smile. I watch as Melissa squirms in her seat. Melissa is attempting to understand the reason for our current seating arrangement. Why did the Order call for this meeting? It's too early to announce nuptials with graduation still far away. We haven't had our annual gala yet. She so fondly loves to remind me that we are about to get married.

"Vikiar!" Riordan calls out. "Begin."

"I want to announce my decision to withdraw from my alliance with Melissa. It is null and void."

She stands. Her mouth is opening and closing as her father looks at me like he wants to murder me with his bare hands.

"How is this possible?" her father asks, bewildered, looking around the room.

"It's simple," Dravin says. "Valen Vikiar is not marrying your daughter."

"Why the hell not?"

"Because she drugged and violated Prey. A Prey that happens to be his wife. It's not the first time she has done it."

"That's a lie," her father bellows.

"It's no secret your daughter is a lesbian," Reid points out. "Ask my wife." Reid glances at Garret. "Ask Garret. We have witnessed her having sex with women."

"You're all a bunch of liars."

The door to the church opens, and Melody walks in, with Rose close behind.

"She can't be here," Garret interjects, pointing directly at Rose.

"She is, and she will stay. She is Prey, and if I want her here, she stays." Garret sits down but glares at Rose.

Melody glances at me, and I smile with pride at my wife. I nod for her to continue.

She opens the leather book from the Order to a page, but I don't miss the darkness in her eyes.

"It says here that if a member causes the death of another, the punishment is death, is it not?"

"It is," Old Man Caruthers chimes in. "Who are you?"

"Mrs. Vikiar. Valen's wife."

"You are a lying bitch!" Melissa screams.

Melody smiles maliciously. I can see the hunger in her eyes. She walks up with a serrated knife and, in one motion, slices Melissa's throat. Blood shoots out like a geyser.

Rose screams in terror.

"Holy shit." Mr. Bedford says in dismay.

"That was for my baby, you bitch. It was you in the room with them." Melody stabs her eyes, and they pop like eggs. Blood is splattering everywhere. She continues to stab her face. Blood continues to squirt for about five minutes.

"Stop her!" her father yells in panic and then tries to grab her, but I'm faster. I shoot him point-blank in the head. He falls over the pew.

I stand. "Touch my wife, and I'll cut you to pieces." I glance at Garret. "Get Rose out of here."

CHAPTER THIRTY ONE

MELODY

"SO HOW ARE YOU, MELODY?" Dr. Wick inquires. "How's school?"

"Three years, and I graduate."

"Good, and married life?"

"Oh, um, okay, I guess."

"You know that you are married, right?"

"Of course," I lie.

She doesn't know which version of me she is talking to right now.

"Hmm...and your boyfriend?"

I smile. "Valen is great. We're good?"

"How about your sister, Rose?"

I pinch my brows. "My sister, Rose?"

"Your sister. She attends Kenyan."

"Rose isn't my sister. Dr. Wick. I just met her."

She smiles like she knows something I don't. Like those pity smiles you give to people who are sick and don't know they are dying.

"You're her only sister, Melody."

"Her sister graduated. My sister's name is Madison."

"Yes, but that is not your biological sister, is it?" I look around the room, and it sways. I feel dizzy. The ground rushes to the ceiling, and everything goes black.

I WAKE up in my Valen's bed—my bed.

"You're awake. Are you okay?"

I place my hand over my forehead. "I had this crazy dream. I was in a psychiatrist's office, and her name was Dr. Wick, and she said Rose was my sister."

He caresses my face and places a soft kiss on my lips. "I love you, Melody." He places the palm of his hand over my belly.

"I love you, too," I confess. I do. I love him.

He smiles. "I've waited a long time for you to say that."

"I'm sorry you had to wait so long."

"It was worth it," he says, caressing my stomach.

"Is my stomach upset?"

"No. It's"—he swallows—"growing."

"What?"

"You're pregnant, Melody. Two months."

He reaches for a book he keeps in the drawer on the nightstand and hands me a sonogram. "I can't believe it. Isn't she beautiful?"

"How do you know it's a she?" I say it with a smile.

I read the sonogram, and I am. I'm pregnant. My heart melts. I see the small pea in the black-and-white picture. Melody Vikiar with my birthdate and the date of the sonogram taken the day of the library. I remember because it was the day he ate my pussy when I was trying to reach for the book.

"Daddies know these things. It's a girl, and I'm going to pay for everything I've done because she is going to bust my balls."

I laugh and place my hand over his while he caresses my stomach. "I love you, Valen."

"And I love you," he says with such depth to his voice.

"What did the doctor mean about Rose?"

He caresses my thigh, making circles with his finger. "You fainted. I guess the stress and the pregnancy. According to the doctor, you can switch at any given time. The safest thing is for you to be aware of everything and everyone."

"It's why you waited."

"If I was going to love you, I needed to love all of you. Every part of your mind and soul. The same way I gave you all of me."

"What about your problem?"

"I get to have two girls with the same name," he teases. "It's enough, trust me."

I snort. "I fuck different or something?"

He stares.

"I do, don't I? Is it bad?"

He shakes his head with a smile. "No. It's fucking crazy and hot as hell."

"Was it you in the woods?"

"You love the mask? The older Melody likes me to fuck her with it."

"The younger one does too."

"Which one..."

"You fucked us both. The beginning was me, and the ending was..."

I close my eyes, and I can see him over there. A memory of that night. The piercings of his cock rubbing between the folds of my pussy. I'm moaning, but the gag is in my mouth, keeping me from screaming. I arch my back, and he is fucking me with two fingers in my ass. I buck when I come, and then he rips his mask off. I can see the sexy smile on his face while a string of spit lands on his gloved hand before he continues to fuck my ass with his fingers.

"What do you remember?"

I open my eyes. "Everything. You fucked me."

His gaze glides over me and says, "Everywhere. I fucked you everywhere for hours."

"And what about Rose?"

He sighs. "Rose is your biological sister, but the sister she thinks graduated died."

My heart breaks. "How?"

"She was in a car accident with her parents, and none of them survived."

"How did she get into Kenyan, and how is Rose my sister?"

"Your mother had two girls. CPS took you both after she abandoned you. I tracked Rose for you because she is your only living family, and I got her a scholarship after she applied ten times when she was seventeen. Rose has an ugly past, Melody. She was sent to foster care and then got a break with a family, but they all died on a trip to visit her here. Rose was adopted like you were, but in her case, happened twice. The sister Rose thinks graduated, died, and she was sent to foster care at seventeen."

"Who adopted Rose? The second time?"

"Garret's family."

That is why she hated Garret. She thinks he was with her sister when his family adopted her.

"Why Garret?"

"Do you have a better option?"

"His parents do whatever he asks. He asked to help a girl in trouble, and they agreed."

"She's sick."

He nods. "Yes, baby. I love you too much to leave her out there all alone like that."

"Thank you," I say softly.

"I think a part of her inside is drawn to you. She loves you, even if she doesn't realize it."

I look down at our hands. "What about Zack and Sam?"

"What do you mean?"

"Where are they?"

He pulls out his phone and hands it to me.

The article reads: There is a heightened police presence in Ohio. Two Ohio students were found decapitated in their car, with their bodies sitting on the hood of the car outside a frat party house with two red Solo cups with HE DID IT written in blood on the windshield. They discovered their heads in the front seat, their eyes severed.

The killer is still at large. Homicide detectives are now calling it a serial killing. The serial killer is targeting college football players. They have no leads, but students are strongly urged to stay vigilant.

I hand it back. "Was it...?"

"You didn't think me and my little brother were going to let it go, did you?"

CHAPTER THIRTY TWO

MELODY

UNDER THE GRAND arches of the church, the air hummed with softness, and the voice of Lana Del Ray's "Say Yes to Heaven" played like an ancient organ.

Stained glass windows, alive with vivid hues of sapphire and crimson, cast a kaleidoscopic light across the stone floor. Between the towering pillars, the guests stand. My parents and Valen's father. My brother and the rest of the founding fathers of the Order.

At the end of the long, petal-strewn aisle stood the altar, bathed in the ethereal glow of candlelight. The shadows flickered and danced, creating a ballet of darkness and light on the ancient walls. Above, the vaulted ceiling soared, whispering echoes of the lyrics as I walked down the aisle.

Valen stands with pride, donned in an elegantly tailored suit of midnight velvet. Azriel stands beside him as the best man.

A hush falls upon the crowd as I take off my gown, which is completely inside a masterpiece of lace and whispers of tulle, trailing me like a silvery mist. My veil, a delicate web of the finest silk, barely conceals the excitement and love in my eyes. With each step, the echo of my heels on the stone sings in rhythm.

The priest stands, with a voice both clear and reverent, as he begins. My husband, breaking tradition, lifts the veil and places a soft kiss on my lips, a seal of love and a promise of forever. The applause renders the priest speechless for a minute.

When it's our Valen's turn to say our vows, He clears his throat with my ring on the tip of my finger. He looks at me with his eyes glistening and begins, "In the quiet shadows of our solitude, we found each other, seeking the part of us that was missing. I vow to be the keeper of your secrets and the partner of your soul. I vow to love you beyond the final breath of stars, in the spaces where darkness whispers its truth. When night falls and the world sleeps, you are my love, and I promise to love every part of you. Where you forget, I'll remember for us both. If you get lost, I promise to bring you back so I can love you harder and longer until we both rest peacefully on earth." He slides the ring the rest of the way. "Forever in your embrace."

My eyes blur. "I do," I say with a smile. "I love you, Valen Vikiar, with everything that I am. Every part of me is yours forever."

THE END
Want more of the Prey Series?
Preorder
Prey Series Book 6
Envy
The Envious... Covet the Prey
2/6/25
Rose and Garret's Story
Don't forget to sign up for my newsletter and follow me on my socials to keep up with all my new releases scan the QR code on the next page.

Check out my alter ego Delilah Croww
Erotic Horror
Whispers in the Dark
Circle of Freaks
www.delilahcroww.com
www.carmenrosales.com
For readers 18+ with no triggers

ABOUT THE AUTHOR

Carmen Rosales is a Latinx author of Steamy, and Dark Romance. She loves spending time with her family. When she is not writing, she is reading. She is an Army veteran and is currently completing her Doctorate Degree in Business and has the love and support of her husband and five children. She also writes under Delilah Croww for her DARK romance horror stories with really dark themes. She loves to see a review and interact with her readers-Join her VIP list- www.carmenrosales.com
.

Scan the QR code to follow her on Social Media, sign up for her Newsletter, and for preorder links for upcoming releases: